My Life As a
Smashed Burrito with
Extra Hot Sauce

the incredible worlds of
Wally McDoogle

My Life As a
Smashed Burrito with
Extra Hot Sauce

BILL MYERS

Illustrations by Jeff Mangiat

Tommy nelson™
A Division of Thomas Nelson, Inc.
www.tommynelson.com
www.ThomasNelson.com

For Terri, Kevin, Apphia, Noel, Tabitha . . .
and, of course, my good buddy, Joe.

"Happy is the person who finds wisdom. And happy is the person who gets understanding. Wisdom is worth more than silver. It brings more profit than gold. Wisdom is more precious than rubies. Nothing you want is equal to it."

—Proverbs 3:13–15

Contents

Chapter 1
Just for Starters

Don't get me wrong, Camp Wahkah Wahkah wasn't the worst experience I've ever had. I mean, when you're the shortest kid in sixth grade, forced to wear Woody Allen glasses all your life, and basically serve as the all-school punching bag, you've got lots of bad experiences to choose from. But Camp Whacko (that's what we called it for short) definitely rated right up there in the top ten.

I knew I was in trouble the moment I stepped onto the camp bus. Of course it was full of the usual screaming crazies. No surprise there. I mean, you take the politest kid in the world and put him on a camp bus, and he goes bonkers. Count on it. It's like a law or something. What caught me off guard was the flying peanut butter and jelly sandwich . . . open faced, of course. I tried to duck, but I was too late.

K-THWACK! right in the old kisser.

Fortunately, the jelly was grape, my favorite. And by the gentle aroma of freshly baked peanuts, I knew the peanut butter had to be Skippy. Another lucky break. What was not lucky was that it completely covered my glasses. I couldn't see a thing.

Before I knew it, the bus ground into gear and lurched forward. Everyone cheered. Well, almost everyone. I was busy stumbling down the aisle at record speed. Of course, there were the usual "Smooth move, Dork Breath" and "Way to go, McDoogle" as I tumbled past. (What a comfort to hear familiar voices in time of trouble.)

Then I got lucky. Through the peanut butter I caught a glimpse of an empty seat toward the back. It took a little doing and bouncing off a couple campers—"Oh, ick!" "Get away, Geek!" (more of my old school chums)—but I finally managed to crash into the empty seat.

Whew. Safe at last. Well, not exactly . . .

As I peeled the bread off my face and removed my glasses, I noticed that the whole bus had grown very quiet. I quickly scraped the peanut butter and jelly gunk off of my glasses and into my hands. Then I pushed my glasses back on.

I wished I hadn't.

The first thing I noticed was that all eyes were on me.

The second thing I noticed was a thick crackly voice. A voice that sounded like it ate gravel for lunch and then washed it down with a box of thumbtacks.

But that was nothing compared to the third thing I noticed—the fierce-sounding, gravelly voice was directed at *ME*.

"You're sitting in my seat."

I turned to see who was talking.

Another mistake. Sometimes if you're going to die, it's best not to know the details. But by recognizing the kid's face and noticing the size of his biceps, I not only knew the "who," I knew the "how."

It was Gary the Gorilla. He hated that name. In fact, he did bodily harm to anyone he heard using it. But it was all anyone knew him by. We'd never officially met, but I recognized his picture from the papers. Or maybe it was the post office. Or maybe both. It didn't matter where. The point is, once you saw it you never forgot it. And you'd always go out of your way to avoid it.

That's okay, I thought. *Don't panic. Turn on some of that world-famous McDoogle charm. Be his friend. Yeah, that's it. The poor guy's probably just misunderstood. Maybe if somebody reached out to him and tried—*

"Hi there," I said, reaching to shake his hand. "My name is Wally McDoogle. I'm, uh . . ."

I don't know whether I stopped because of the look on his face or the gasps from the crowd. But when I glanced down at our handshake, I saw the problem. I had just transferred all of the peanut butter and jelly gunk from my hand into his.

"Oh, sorry, Mr. Gorilla, . . . er, that is, I mean . . ."

With one swift move he had me by the collar. Next, I was high above his head and pressed tightly to the ceiling of the bus.

Suddenly, my whole life passed before my eyes. Well, it wasn't my whole life. Mostly just the part of how I got into this predicament. It all started with Dad less than eight weeks ago . . .

"Don't worry," he shouted, leaning over the lawn mower as I fought to empty the grass catcher. "Church camp will be great for you."

"But Dad—"

"Especially that two-day canoe trip—get you out in the wild away from the luxuries of the big city—"

"But Dad—"

"New challenges, new adventures—"

"Dad."

"And the most important thing of all . . ."

Uh-oh, I thought, *here it comes.*

"It will make you a real man."

"*A real man.*" That seemed to be Dad's whole purpose in my life lately. Maybe it had to do with him being All-State something or other back in his high school football days. Or maybe it was because Burt and Brock, my older twin brothers, win every sports trophy they can get their sweaty paws on. Or maybe it was because I made the mistake of telling everybody at dinner one night that I wanted to be a writer.

"A writer?" Dad winced.

"Yeah, but not just a writer—a *screen*writer. You know, like movies and stuff."

"Yeah, but . . . *a writer?*" The word stuck in his throat like Aunt Martha's overcooked chicken.

"Sure, lots of people do that."

"But . . . a writer?"

Less than four weeks later, the brochure from Camp Whacko mysteriously showed up on my dresser. It wasn't long before the camp found its way into our daily conversations. It made no difference how I argued. Somehow, someway, just four weeks later, I found myself loading my bags into the car and heading for the church bus.

"You sure you need that computer thing?" Dad asked as he suspiciously eyed the laptop computer I was carrying to the car.

"Sure Dad." I tried to sound matter of fact. "It will, uh, um, it will help me take notes on all the outdoorsy stuff I learn."

"Hmmm . . ." was all he said.

I pulled the computer closer to my side. This could get messy.

He stood beside the car and slowly crossed his arms.

"Please, God," I silently prayed, *"not Ol' Betsy, too."* ("Betsy," that's what I call my computer.)

Finally, Mom spoke up. "I think he should take it, Herb. It's one thing to ship the boy off to camp against his will, but to take away his computer?"

"I didn't say we should," Dad hedged. "It's just with all the new experiences he'll be having, I wonder if it's really necessary to—"

"I *really* think he should take it, Herb."

Now, everyone in our family knows what it means when Mom says *"really"* like that. It means her mind is made up. Oh sure, Dad could still have his way—after all, he is the man of the house. But if he did, it meant he'd have to pay for it in the days to come. Little things like cold dinners, burnt toast, or finding starch in his underwear. You know, details like that.

"It was just a suggestion," he offered as he threw the rest of my bags into the trunk.

"Thanks, Mom." I grinned and climbed into the car.

"No sweat, Kiddo," she said, sticking her head through the open window and giving me a good-bye kiss. "But you owe me."

"Put it on my bill."

Dad started the car, but before we pulled away, Mom went down her list of usual "Mom" things. You know, stuff like, "I expect you to wear your pajamas. Tops *and* bottoms."

"Yes, Mom."

"And don't forget to change your underwear."

"Yes, Mom."

"And don't forget to floss. Remember, healthy gums are happy gums."

"Son . . ." Now it was Dad's turn. But instead of a long lecture he reached over, put his powerful hand on my shoulder, and looked me straight in the eyes. I knew it was going to be something profound, something deeply moving, something I'd remember the rest of my life.

"Son," he repeated to build the suspense. Then after a deep breath he continued. "Think . . . *manly* thoughts."

I did my best to smile. He gave me a reassuring nod, put the car in gear, and off we headed for the bus.

That was just half an hour ago. And now, thirty short minutes later, I was pinned to the roof of the bus by Gary the Gorilla.

So this is what it feels like to die? I thought. *Not so bad. Course, it would be better if he'd let go of my collar so I could breathe. Still, on the McDoogle pain scale of 1 to 10 this is only a—*

Suddenly, an idea came to mind. I reached down to his meaty hand (the one wrapped around my throat) and scraped the rest of the peanut butter and jelly from it. Next I began to eat the stuff. The idea was to get him to laugh, to show him that I was just a stupid geek and that this was all just a stupid geek accident.

Unfortunately, he didn't laugh. But the rest of the bus did. And as they chuckled, Gary, being the insecure kind of bully he was, naturally thought they were laughing at him.

His grip around my neck tightened.

Now, I've got to admit, I don't exactly remember praying. Sometimes when you're busy dying you forget little details like that. But suddenly, out of the blue, I heard this voice:

"Put him down, Gary."

At first I thought it was God, or at least one of those archangel guys we hear about in Sunday school. After all, this was a church bus going to a church camp. But when I turned I saw it was only a counselor. Still, beggars can't be choosers. I'd take what I could get.

Gary gave the man a glare but the counselor stayed cool and calm.

"Put him down," the man repeated.

I gave my glasses a nervous little push back onto my nose. Unfortunately, it was with the hand still dripping in peanut butter and jelly. I noticed an exceptionally large glob of the goo starting to fall. I tried to catch it but I was too late.

K-SPLAT!

From high above it nailed Gorilla Boy right in the ol' face.

The bus broke into even louder laughter.

Gary never had people laugh at him—at least not to his face—at least no one who lived to tell about it. And to have it happen twice in a row was unthinkable. But instead of enjoying the experience as something to treasure and remember, Gary turned beet red. The muscles in his neck began to tighten and quiver. He turned to the rest of the bus and gave them his world-famous death glare.

The rest of the bus stopped laughing. Come to think of it, they may have stopped breathing.

Finally, the counselor's voice broke the silence. "It's the last time I'm telling you, Gary . . . put him down."

Slowly, Gary turned his head and directed his death glare at me. I could almost feel the plastic rims of my glasses melting.

Then he dropped me. I hit the floor like a sack of potatoes. But at least a living sack of potatoes. For that I was grateful.

I was not grateful for Gary's final words to me. "I'm not going to forget this, Weasel. No one makes a fool of me. *No one*."

Chapter 2

New Friends/ Old Enemies

Three hours later we pulled into Camp Whacko. We hopped from the bus and hauled our junk off to our luxurious cabins—complete with rusting bunk beds, squeaky bed springs, and paper-thin mattresses. It didn't look like sleep would be a high priority. But that's okay. I planned to spend the nights counting all the different six-legged wildlife scurrying across the floor, anyway.

After settling in, we all met at the softball bleachers. I did my best to sit as far away from Gary and his two goon friends as possible. But by the way they kept whispering and glaring at me, I figured China would have been too close.

The counselor guy who saved my life—Dale was his name—did most of the talking. He went on about how much fun we were going to have at Camp Whacko. You know, the standard, run-of-the-mill "I'm glad you're all here" and "we're all going to have a great time" sort of stuff.

Then he talked about the overnight canoe trip coming up in a few days. And finally he got around to the week's theme. "For the next five days we're going to learn all about wisdom. Isn't that exciting?"

Guess again. More like five days of nonstop boredom. No offense, but I'd only heard them rattle on about wisdom a billion times in Sunday school. That didn't stop ol' Dale, though. He just went on rattling. "Wisdom is knowing right from wrong. It's learning what God's will is and then doing it. Now, can anybody here give me an example?"

A hundred hands shot up—mostly belonging to the younger crowd . . . mostly belonging to the girls who all had instant, heartbreaking crushes on the guy.

I tried my best to pay attention, but no sale. I'd heard it all before. So I reached down to Ol' Betsy, my laptop computer. I quietly popped open her lid and snapped her on. Her screen started to glow, and I started to think.

There has to be some way of making this wisdom stuff more interesting. If I could just come up with the right story. Then before I knew it, my fingers started to fly across the keyboard. . . .

It has been a long afternoon for our superhero. Already, Mutant Man McDoogle has stopped a runaway train, saved the earth from a cloud of giant asteroids, and cleaned out the family's cat box.

And now to the biggest challenge of all—complex fractions. (Being a sixth-grade superhero with homework does have its disadvantages.) Grabbing his pencil and math book, he snaps on the ol' tube for a little Brady Bunch rerun inspiration. Suddenly, right in the middle of "Here's a story, of a lovely lady..." the TV picture breaks up. Instead of Marsha and the gang giving their cute little smiles and their cute little waves from their cute little boxes we see...Dr. Ghastly the gorilla!

No one's sure where the gorilla got his smarts or why he used them for such evil purposes. Some say it was after eating too many bananas with those little round stickers still on them. Others say it was after being exposed to seventy-two hours of nonstop rap music. Then there's the theory of his mom never buying him brand-name clothes.

Whatever the reason, after breaking out of the Brooklyn Zoo (and taking a few night courses at Harvard), Dr. Ghastly

set up his secret underground labora-
tory. Here he became the most feared
(and hairiest) scientist of all time.

But, back to our story...

"Mutant Man," the gorilla sneers
as only the world's slyest and most
sinister scientist can sneer, "I know
you're out there."

Our hero stares at the TV screen and
gasps a manly gasp.

"I thought you might want to know...
I've just created another one of my
little inventions," says Dr. Ghastly.

The TV picture grows wider. We see
this baddest of all bad guys (or
guyettes for that matter) standing
beside a giant vacuum cleaner.

"It's my Handy Dandy Wisdom Sucker
Upper. All I do is flip this little
switch." He reaches over to snap it
on. "And it begins to suck up all of
the world's wisdom." Dr. Ghastly
laughs his sinister jungle laugh,
"Oo-oo-ah-ah-ee-ee," and suddenly
disappears from the screen.

A searing pain rips into our superhero's manly jaw. "Augh! My wisdom
teeth!" he cries. "They're gone!"

But, alas, it's not just his wisdom teeth. Every wisdom tooth in the world has been stolen. Fearing the worst, he spins around to the nativity scene left over from last Christmas. Just as he suspects. The Three Wise Men have also disappeared.

"Great Scott! Everything to do with wisdom is being sucked into the machine! This sounds like a job for...Ta-Da-Daaaa (that, of course is superhero music)... Mutant Man McDoogle!"

He presses the button on his secret Muton-Belt. Suddenly, his mighty powers are released. With one giant step his rubberized legs reach out the door, stretch down three flights of stairs and into the street. A neat trick. Unfortunately, it always means having his mom buy him a new pair of jeans.

Outside it's worse than he suspects. Everywhere people are acting crazy. Cars honking and plowing into each other. Decent, law-abiding folks screaming and beating up other decent, law-abiding folks. I mean, it's worse than Christmas shopping at the mall. Well, maybe not that bad, but close.

"People! People, you must stop this at once!" Mutant Man shouts.

But nobody listens. He grabs a passing mother who's stuffing her mouth full of chocolate. "It's Dr. Ghastly! Don't you understand? He's taking all your wisdom!"

But Mom won't listen. She's too busy shouting at her kid who's also gobbling up candy. "Hurry and eat!" she screams at the child. "If we don't finish off this case of Three Musketeers before dinner, we won't spoil our appetites!"

"It's no use, Mutant Mind!"

Our hero snaps his handsome head up to see the gruesome gorilla. He is circling in a helicopter high overhead. Behind him trails the Wisdom Sucker Upper... still sucking up.

The hairy ape continues his threats. "Soon all wisdom will be mine!" he shouts through the loudspeakers. "Soon the entire world will be in total chaos. Oo-oo-ah-ah-ee-ee..."

"Not if I can help it!" our hero shouts. Then with a mighty deep breath (the type that only superheros can breathe...so don't try this at home,

kids), Mutant Man begins a little sucking of his own.

His tremendous lungs pull in all of
the surrounding air. And with that air
comes the helicopter. Try as he might,
Dr. Ghastly can't pull away. Our hunk
of a hero is sucking too hard. Closer
and closer the chopper comes.

"Let me go!" Dr. Ghastly cries. "Let
me go!"

But our hero doesn't let go. He continues to inhale. And the helicopter
continues to be sucked in.

But, alas and alack, it's been a
long day, and Mutant Man begins to grow
weary—not to mention a little dizzy.
He has no choice. Our incurably handsome hero must stop.

Still, all is not lost...

He makes one of his world-famous jumps
toward the helicopter. Unfortunately, he
only soars two or three hundred feet into
the air. (Like I said, he's a bit tuck-
ered.) He nearly misses but not quite.
After all, he is the hero of the story.
In the final second, his arm stretches
the last fifty feet, and he manages to
grab the chopper's landing skids.

Still, ol' Ghastly has more than a hairy elbow up his sleeve. Suddenly, he throws the helicopter into reverse.

"Look out!" the crowd screams from below.

Mutant Man turns just in time to see the 203-story Bank of Africa building coming straight at him. "What luck!" our hero cries. "This must be where Dr. Ghastly banks! Maybe he's stopping to take out a little money!" But in a second he realizes Dr. Ghastly is not making a withdrawal. It's more like a deposit. And not a deposit of money but of Mutant Man...right against the side of the building.

They race toward the bank at lightning speed.

"Come on, Doctor!" our hero shouts nervously. "Stop monkeying around."

But the gorilla has gone ape. He will not listen. He is set on smashing Mutant Man into the side of the building.

By now the bank is so close our hero can see the horrified expressions of the people inside.

Oh no! What will happen? What will the incredibly groomed and well-flossed

Mutant Man do? How will he get out of this one?

Then suddenly—

"Hey, Wally, put that computer away and get ready for lunch!"

It was Dale.

Rats, I hate it when that happens. Every time I get to a good part in one of my stories, somebody has to interrupt me. But I figured this interruption was for a good cause. I mean, he did say "lunch," right?

I pressed F10 and shut Ol' Betsy down for a while. I figured I'd have plenty of time to get back to Mutant Man and Dr. Ghastly the gorilla . . . that is, if the real Gary Gorilla didn't get me first. . . .

* * * * *

The three of us stumbled out of the cafeteria. The "cafeteria" is what the counselors called it. But by now we'd all given it another name . . . "The Toxic Waste Site." The only thing decent to eat were the half-frozen burritos. Well, they weren't supposed to be half-frozen, but the cook wasn't crazy about slaving over a hot oven, so there they were, direct from the freezer and onto our plates. The trick was to think of them as cheese and bean popsicles instead of burritos. And with the extra hot sauce poured on top, they were actually pretty good—weird, but good. I was busy crunching away on my third one as we staggered out the doors.

"You call that a lunch?" Wall Street groaned, holding her stomach. She was a Latino girl about my age.

"What were those hard blue things?" I asked.

"Mashed potatoes!" Opera shouted. "Or butter balls!"

I threw a look over at the chubby kid beside us. Even though his Walkman was cranked up to ten, it's like he could still hear. Either that or he was the world's greatest lip reader. Amazing. Right then he had been listening to "Barber of Seville" by Fetuccine or Tortellini or one of those opera-type guys.

"How can you stand to listen to that junk?" Wall Street shouted. "You can't even understand the words."

"Can you understand today's stuff?" Opera shouted back.

Wall Street gave a shrug.

"So what's the difference?"

He had her there.

The three of us had met at lunch. Opera and I were the first to spot each other. Immediately, we recognized the other guy for what he was . . . a fellow "Dorkoid."

DORKOIDS. You know the type. While everyone else is wearing hot new fashions, we're sporting frozen-oldie hand-me-downs. While everyone else has these terrific put-downs, we usually say something stupid or, worse yet, polite. And while everyone else's chests begin looking like Sylvester Stalone (if you're a guy) and Marilyn Monroe (if you're a girl), we just keep on looking like Pee Wee Herman and, well, Pee Wee Herman.

Like I said, Opera and I were the first to meet. Wall Street didn't join our little club until the meal was nearly over.

"You almost missed lunch," I said as she sat beside us.

"I'll try harder next time," she joked, poking at the frozen burrito on her plate.

"I think they're hot dogs," Opera shouted over his Walkman.

"Or giant caterpillars. It's hard to tell when they're frozen like that." I shrugged.

"Thanks for the warning."

"How come you were so late?" I asked.

"I was looking for an electrical outlet—there aren't any in the cabins."

"Why do you need an electrical outlet?" Opera shouted.

"To recharge my cell phone," she said.

I gave Opera a look. It sounded like the Dork-oids were about to increase membership by one. I was almost afraid to ask the question, but I knew somebody had to. "So . . . what do you need a cell phone for?"

"Why do you need a computer?" she countered.

"I'm going to be a screenwriter."

"And I'm going to be a stockbroker."

"Maybe we should start charging dues," I muttered.

"Pardon me?"

"Never mind." I grinned as I reached out to shake her hand. "Welcome aboard." I wasn't sure what type of stock a ten-year-old girl could buy and sell, but that didn't make much difference. The point was, she definitely qualified for membership.

Fifteen minutes later, the three of us crossed the courtyard toward our cabins. We were friends forever . . . or at least until the end of the week, whichever came first.

And then it happened . . .

Suddenly, Gary and his two Goons showed up behind us. They didn't say a word. Neither did we. In fact, everything got very, very quiet. Everything except Opera's Walkman. At that moment some fat lady was screaming her lungs out like she was about to die.

How appropriate, I thought.

We continued to walk, and they continued to follow. Other kids also started following. Like vultures they all seemed to know when someone was about to meet their Maker.

Soon we (and most of the camp) arrived at our cabin. But I'd had enough. I mean, if I was going to die, I might as well do it now before I had to face another meal at the Toxic Waste Site.

Well, here goes, I figured. *It's now or never.* Suddenly, I turned around. "Oh, hi, Gary." I pretended to be surprised. "So how's it going, man?" I raised my hand to give him a high five. But instead of slapping my hand, he just looked it over, probably checking for more peanut butter and jelly.

Everyone waited. There was only silence . . . except for the fat lady singing.

Finally, Goon One cleared his throat. "In the spirit of friendship, different groups are chipping in to help Gary out on his chores." Maybe it was just my imagination, but suddenly the kid started to sound like one of those guys from the gangster movies.

"The Babes are doing Kitchen Duty on his day to do that. The Jocks are carrying his stuff on the canoe trip. And the Eggheads are going to pick up his outdoor garbage. So that just leaves you guys—the Dorkoids."

"What's left?" Wall Street asked hesitantly. "There's nothing left, is there?"

"Latrine Duty," Goon One said with a grin.

The rest of the camp gave a little chuckle.

"But there's no Latrine Duty," Opera shouted. The fat lady was singing even louder than before. "Every cabin has to clean their own bathroom."

Gary just gave him a look.

"Well, that's the truth," Opera shouted. "Those are the rules. We can't go against the rules."

But Gary wasn't much interested in rules. He suddenly ripped off Opera's headphones, threw them to the dirt, and ground them under his foot.

The fat lady died sooner than we had hoped.

For a moment Opera just stared down at the remains. Then, when we were sure he was about to break into a good case of tears, he looked up at Gary, gave a loud sniff, and *threw himself at him*—all 187 pounds worth!

The crowd gasped at Opera's stupidity. This was going to be better than they'd hoped.

Of course, Gary easily sidestepped Opera and had him in an armlock faster than you could say, "Oh well, nice try." But the Gorilla wasn't finished. In true bully fashion, he threw Opera to Goon

Two, who tossed him to the ground and started yanking his arm back even further. Feeling a little left out, Goon One also joined in.

Opera screamed in pain and for good reason. I had no idea arms could bend so far back. Without stopping to think, I suddenly leaped at the Goons and tried to pry them off. I would have had them too—if I wasn't holding the burrito in my hand and if I wasn't outweighed by a few hundred pounds. Finally, one of them grabbed me by the shoulder and sent me spinning right back into my ol' buddy Gary.

For a moment the expression in Gary's eyes was shock. I didn't understand—until I looked lower and saw my smashed burrito with extra hot sauce smeared all across his neck and chin.

By now the whole camp was there, and in a second everybody was laughing.

Not great news. Gary was still a little sensitive in the "Being Laughed At Department."

Then someone began to clap. And then another. And then another. Before we knew it everyone in the camp was laughing and clapping.

Everyone but Gary . . . and me.

Ever so slowly Gary reached up and wiped the burrito goop off his neck. Then he smashed the goop right into the center of my chest—a little harder than I felt necessary to make his point.

Next, he clenched his right fist. *Uh-oh,* I thought, *here it comes: a little free dental work.* But then, just before he let loose, I heard:

"That's enough, Gary."

It was Dale. All right, Dale! The guy was getting pretty good at this rescue business.

Gary slowly turned around. He was obviously taller than Dale—by a good three inches. And we're not talking three inches of fat. We're talking muscle—major muscle.

But Dale wouldn't back down. "I said that's enough."

Gary eyeballed him for a long minute, trying his best to scare the guy. But Dale didn't budge. Not an inch. Finally, with a heavy snort, Gary let go of my shirt. "That's three, Weasel," he snarled at me under his breath. "I owe you for three."

(Actually, I figured it was only two. The bus and here. But hey, with his muscles, I guess the guy didn't have to be a math whiz.)

Still, that wasn't the worst. For as Gary and his Goon Patrol turned to leave, the rest of the crowd started to chant . . . *"Wal-ly, Wal-ly, Wal-ly . . ."*

I guess they thought it was pretty funny.

Not me. Because with each *"Wal-ly,"* I knew I'd be feeling even greater pain from the Gorilla. Sure, maybe not at that moment, but let's face it, there's no way Dale could keep showing up all the time.

Meanwhile, Opera rose to his feet and started comparing the lengths of his arms.

"Come on," I mumbled, "let's get out of here."

All this as the crowd continued to chant: *"Wal-ly, Wal-ly, Wal-ly . . ."*

* * * * *

I changed T-shirts back at the cabin. For a long moment, I held the one with the burrito and hot sauce smeared all over the front. As I stood there, I couldn't help but make the comparison. Somehow I figured that burrito goop symbolized my whole life at Camp Whacko. "A smashed burrito," I mumbled half aloud. "Now doesn't that just figure . . . a smashed burrito with extra hot sauce."

Chapter 3

Testing ...
One, Two, Three

The rest of the day went off pretty smooth. We managed to survive another meal at the Toxic Waste Site. I managed to stay out of Gary's way. And that evening Dale even managed to give a pretty good talk. Don't get me wrong, it was still about wisdom and stuff, but somehow it started to make more sense. Mostly it was about how it's wise to choose good friends.

"Be with wise men and become wise," he read from somewhere in the Bible. "Be with evil men and become evil."

Like I said, it made pretty good sense. Course, I wanted to add a couple of my own verses, like . . .

"Be with Dorkoids and become a Dorkoid."
"Be with Gary the Gorilla and become dead."

But seriously, Dale had a point. Since you become like the people you hang out with, why not hang out with the good guys? Plain and simple, right?

I just wished I could have remembered how plain and simple it was a couple of hours later.

Wall Street had come over to our cabin. The three of us sat out on the porch and talked about a lot of nothing. But that's okay, sitting around talking about a lot of nothing with friends is a lot better than talking about a lot of something with strangers. (Whatever that means.)

Anyway, everyone else was down at the snack bar trying to wash the taste of dinner out of their mouths. Or they were up at the video games trying to save the universe from the latest Space-Droids. Then of course there were the usual handful who were somewhere out in the bushes practicing the highly overrated and germ-infested art of making out.

But not us. We were having an in-depth conversation about a major world problem—what we were going to wear on the canoe trip—when suddenly the bushes near the cabin started to rustle.

"Did you hear that?" Wall Street asked, lowering her voice.

We nodded in silence.

The rustling grew louder.

"Do you think it's HIM?" I whispered.

"Don't . . . don't be stupid," Opera stuttered.

"Great, then, if it's not HIM, why don't you go out and see who it is," I suggested.

Opera gave me a glare.

Now by *HIM* we're talking about the local Camp Mauler. I suppose every camp has one. You know, some local monster who lurks in the woods just past the lights. Usually, they're big and hairy and just dying to gobble up poor, unsuspecting kids who haven't gotten back to their cabin by Lights Out.

Of course, we all knew he was make-believe— probably created by the counselors to keep everyone in bed. So, of course, none of us were really frightened of him. But still, when it comes to monsters, you can never be too careful.

There was more rustling and now some cracking of twigs. He was nearly on top of us. No doubt about it. One more step and we'd be some monster's late-night snack!

At last the time came. I could wait no longer. I mean, a man's gotta do what a man's gotta do. I grabbed my hands, squeezed hard, and began to crack my knuckles.

My friends scowled at me. But I had no choice. When I get nervous, I crack my knuckles. It's like a habit or something. It's also the best relaxer there is. Forget the tranquilizers, forget the self-help books, forget the counseling sessions. Just take up knuckle cracking.

Snap-pop, snap-pop, snap-pop . . .

Wall Street and Opera kept glaring. I mean, if looks could kill, I'd be dead. But before they could decide on the method of execution, the bushes finally flew apart. And suddenly, in all his awesomeness, appeared . . .

Jimmy Jack Hucksterly.

"Hey, McDoogle, my man," he said, shaking the pine needles from his oily black hair. "How's it going?"

"Jimmy Jack," I sighed in relief. "It's only you."

I knew Jimmy Jack from school. And, though he wasn't the monster we feared, I should have been more careful. You see, wherever he went, Jimmy Jack was bad news. It's not that he was a bully or anything like that. In fact, he was one of the few people in the world shorter than me. But Jimmy Jack Hucksterly had a reputation—a reputation as wide as the gap between his front teeth.

Jimmy Jack was always on the make. Selling this, selling that, making this deal, making that deal. Nothing wrong with that. But somehow Jimmy Jack always got the better end of the deal . . . even if it meant a little lying. Even if it meant a *lot* of lying.

The point is, people always felt ripped off by Jimmy Jack Hucksterly. And for good reason . . . they usually were.

"McDoogle, listen." He glanced around to make sure no one was listening. Since Opera and Wall Street were Dorkoids, I guess he figured they didn't count. "There's been a lot of talk in camp tonight."

"'Bout what?"

"About your standing up to the Gorilla."

"Hey, I didn't do that on purpose. That was just an acciden—"

"No, no," he interrupted. "I don't mean today, I mean in the future. I mean, for you to stand up to the Gorilla for the rest of us and put a stop to him."

"What do you mean, *'the rest of us'?*"

"The campers, man—all of us. That creep's got us all under his thumb, making us work for him like slaves."

"So?"

"So we need a leader like you to rally the troops and stop him."

"Right, me, the leader."

"No, I'm serious, man. The guy's a disease . . . and you, you're the cure."

"You been watching too many movies, Jimmy Jack." I knew I couldn't trust this guy. Nobody could. Still, if only a few of the kids believed what he said they believed . . . well, that was still kind of neat. In fact, it was so neat that I started to forget what Dale had said. Something about watching who we hang out with, wasn't it? Probably. But at that moment I couldn't exactly remember. And the more I listened to Jimmy Jack, the more I forgot.

That was my first mistake—but not my last.

"Listen to me." Jimmy Jack lowered his voice and moved in closer like we were suddenly best of friends. "We need you, man. If enough of us got behind you—and with me at your side—we could *exterminate* this insect once and for all."

For the next half-hour Jimmy Jack kept working on me. Talk about insects, this guy was like a pesky fly. No matter how many times I waved him away, he just kept coming back. Of course, I didn't say yes to his offer. That would have been suicide. But by the end of the evening, I wasn't exactly saying no, either. And that was mistake number two.

Later, as I lay in bed, I reached for Betsy and snapped her on. I hoped getting back to Mutant Man would help clear my mind. . . .

When we last left our hugably handsome and perfectly straight-toothed hero he was about to make an impression upon the Bank of Africa. A big impression. Like with his whole body. But suddenly, an incredible idea comes to his magnificently mighty mind.

He lets go of the helicopter and falls faster than a kid's smile after learning he's having liver and onions for dinner. Faster and faster he falls. And then faster some more.

But Mutant Man is not worried. Why should he be? After all, he's already read this story. He knows that just thirty feet below are his two faithful sidekicks, Opera and Wall Street.

Disguised as window washers, they've been waiting on their washing platform for hours just in case something like this should happen.

K-Bang, Crash, Crack!

Our hero hits the platform hard. But this is no time to count broken legs... or necks. Mutant Man has a world to save. And, as usual, he'll save it magnificently. Faster than you can say, "Oh no, now what's he up to?" Mutant Man shouts, "Quick, Plan 243½!"

Now as everyone knows, Plan 243½ is the plan for changing window-washing platforms into supersonic jet fighters.

An impossibility?

Perhaps for you, my dear, untrained reader. But not for the likes of the

great Opera and Wall Street. After
all, changing window-washing platforms
into jet fighters was one of the first
things they learned while at Mutant
Man's School of Superherohood.

Soon the puny platform is transformed
into an awesome airplane—complete with
salted peanuts and an in-flight movie
for longer trips.

"Oh no!" Opera suddenly screams, "we
forgot the engine!"

"Don't worry," Wall Street shouts as
she begins digging in her purse. In-
stantly, she pulls out a portable hair
dryer.

"A perfect engine!" Mutant Man cries.
"Strap it onto the back."

In no time flat our hero is ready.
He revs his engine up to "Super-Blow"
and roars into the wild blue yonder,
leaving his two superhelpers behind.

Dr. Ghastly is high overhead. If
Mutant Man can just get closer. If he
can just get the Wisdom Sucker Upper
into his sights and blow a hole in it.
Then all the wisdom would fall back to
earth where it belongs. An easy plan,
right?

Unfortunately, there's a fly in the ointment...literally.

No one saw the little fly sneak on board. But then again, we're not just talking any fly here. We're talking the world-famous Jimmy Jack Jive Fly. As a visitor from the planet MakeUaDeal, this little alien quickly became a friend of used-car salesmen and politicians around the world. And for good reason.

Talk about a fast talker. I mean, this guy could sell you anything—even the shirt off his back. And that's a neat trick since flies never wear shirts (usually just pullover sweaters)...and neater still 'cause if they did wear shirts they'd all have six sleeves in them, and what could you do with a six-sleeved shirt anyway, hmm?

"Pssst...Hey, Mutant. Mutant Man."

Unfazed by his new companion, Mutant Man does his best to be polite. "Oh, it's you. I'm sorry, Mr. Jive Fly, but I haven't time to talk. You see, at the moment, I'm busy saving the world."

"But this is important—really important."

"I'm sure it is, but I already have a closet full of six-sleeved sweaters, I really don't need any—"

"No man, I'm talkin' about ol' Ghastly up ahead."

Our hero does his best to ignore the insect. But the little bug just keeps on...ahem, "bugging" him.

"For just $29.95 I'll sell you this new and improved Hyper Space Map. It shows how to time warp around Jupiter and be at Dr. Ghastly's side in seconds flat."

But Mutant Man is no fool. "Twenty-nine dollars and ninety-five cents! I can get it for half that at K-Mart!"

"All right, all right. I'll give it to you at half price. But only 'cause we're almost at the end of this chapter and don't have time to argue."

"Sold."

In a flash, Mutant hands over the money and enters in the new coordinates. And in a flashier flash, they are lost somewhere around the moons of Jupiter. Well, not really "they." More like "he." You see, ol' Jimmy Jack Jive Fly bailed out at the last second. He knew Mutant

Man wouldn't be thrilled to learn he'd
only bought half a map. And, as we all
know, you only get halfway with half a
map. But at half price, what did the guy
expect?

So now our hero is stranded at the
outer edges of the Solar System. Oh no!
What will he do? How will he ever get
home? And, most importantly, will that
in-flight movie be any good?

Then, suddenly—

"Okay, McDoogle, lights out."

It sounded like the cabin counselor meant
business. So I closed Ol' Betsy's lid, pulled up
the covers, and stared at the ceiling.

Course, I wouldn't be able to sleep. How
could I? The real Jimmy Jack's words still rang
in my mind. Who knows . . . maybe I could be a
hero. Maybe I could free the camp from the
awful dictator-like rule of Gary the Gorilla.

Hmm. . . .

Chapter 4

More Wisdom Bites the Dust

Jimmy Jack Hucksterly worked on me all the next morning. He worked on me as I walked to breakfast. He worked on me as I ate breakfast. He even worked on me as I headed to the bathroom. The guy just wouldn't let up.

"I've spread the word, man. Everyone's waiting. Just say when."

"When what?" I asked, nervously pushing up my glasses.

"When you want the big meeting."

I had started to wear down. I could feel it. Maybe he was right. Maybe being the camp hero was my destiny. But something still didn't feel right.

Later, we were all practicing at the archery range. (If you can call hitting everything but the target "practicing.") I asked Opera and Wall Street what they thought. Opera had sort of managed to repair his Walkman. "Sort of" meaning he only had one earpiece and the tape sounded like it was playing underwater. But with his kind of music, who could tell?

"The guy's bad news!" Opera shouted.

"What about the Gorilla?" I asked. "Somebody's got to stand up to Gary."

"Remember what Dale said," Wall Street reminded me. "About choosing quality friends?"

"So?"

"So I don't think Jimmy Jack Hucksterly exactly qualifies."

I gave Wall Street a long look before grabbing another arrow. Maybe she was right. I pulled back my bow, took aim, and suddenly dropped my mouth open in shock. While we were talking someone had tacked a huge crayon drawing of a gorilla on my target. And you didn't have to be a rocket scientist to figure out who that *who* was.

By lunch it finally happened. Jimmy Jack had finally worn me down. "All right, already, we'll have your stupid meeting!" I sighed. "But just one."

* * * * *

"It's only a meeting," I told Opera on the way back from the arts and crafts room. "I figure three, maybe four kids will show at tops."

"So why even go?!" he shouted over his music.

"So Jimmy Jack will leave me alone."

Eventually, we arrived at the cabin, and I opened the door.

The place was packed.

"I've organized them in groups," Jimmy Jack beamed. "The Eggheads are here to the left."

A half-dozen brainy types nodded at me.

"The Babes are over here."

Nearly a dozen girls grinned and waved from the center of the room. "Hi, Wally . . ."

"The Jocks are here."

"Yo!"

"And your Dorkoids are right behind you."

I turned to see Opera and Wall Street. They both kind of gave sheepish shrugs as if to say, "Oh well, why not?"

For a second I got all shaky. I didn't know what to say or what to do. But that didn't seem to matter, 'cause by the look of things, Jimmy Jack did.

"These are your assignments," he said, passing out photocopied sheets (complete with diagrams) to each of the groups. "Learn them, memorize them, make them your life. If we're to destroy the Gorilla's cruel dictatorship, allowing the downtrodden to rise up in victory, then we must all do our share."

"Cruel dictatorship? Downtrodden rise up in victory?" This guy had DEFINITELY been seeing

too many movies. But when I looked around the cabin everybody nodded as if they understood.

"And now a word from our leader . . ."

All eyes turned toward me. Everyone broke into applause.

I broke into a sweat. They clapped louder. I sweated harder. How'd I know what to say? This was all Jimmy Jack's doing, not mine. But you couldn't convince them of that. No sir, these folks were definitely expecting a hero.

Finally, they settled down and waited for some awe-inspiring words of courage from me. I pushed my glasses back up my nose and smiled. They waited. I smiled harder. They waited longer.

Oh well, I figured, *here goes nothing.* And I couldn't have been more right. I opened my mouth and tried to speak, but no words came. My mouth was as dry as the Sahara Desert. Come to think of it, that was about how empty my brain was, too.

I tried again. Still nothing.

There were a couple uneasy coughs and a few nervous shufflings. I took a deep breath and tried one last time. Then suddenly, as luck would have it, my eyes landed on my T-shirt—the one stained with beans, cheese, and hot sauce. It was hanging above my bunk, drying out from my last run-in with Gary. And before I could stop it, the phrase, "Remember the burrito!" leaped out of my mouth.

Everyone stared in stunned silence.

Jimmy Jack, too. But only for a second. Suddenly, he began to clap. "That's right!" he shouted as he pretended to get excited. "That's great!" he cried. He kept right on clapping and pretty soon others started to clap too. They weren't exactly sure why. But since Jimmy Jack was so excited, they figured they better be.

"Remember the burrito!" Jimmy Jack cried. He began repeating the phrase over and over again, "Remember the burrito! Remember the burrito!"

Others joined in, "Remember the burrito! Remember the burrito!" Soon the entire cabin was chanting, "Remember the burrito! Remember the burrito!"

Granted it wasn't as good as "Remember the Alamo" or any of those other catchy war cries. But it was all I could come up with on such short notice.

"Remember the burrito! Remember the burrito! Remember the burrito!" everyone kept shouting as they headed for the door, as they slapped me on the back, as they thanked me for being such a brilliant leader.

"Remember the burrito?" Jimmy Jack whispered scornfully into my ear. "Give me a break, McDoogle."

But for everybody else, he pretended to smile.

And for everybody else, I pretended to smile back. Still, there was no missing the heavy feeling down in my gut. But it wasn't from the lame slogan. It was something deeper. What had I done? What had I gotten myself into?

All this as the crowd continued cheering and slapping me on the back. "Remember the burrito! Remember the burrito! Remember the burrito! . . ."

* * * * *

An hour later we were all sitting on the bleachers. The afternoon sun felt good and warm on our backs. Dale was giving another one of his talks on wisdom. It was all about how it's wise to be kind to others. It wasn't a bad talk. I mean, on the McDoogle Scale of Boredom it was only about a 2.4.

He went on about how we should all be nice to everybody. No matter who they were, we should be kind to everybody. I figured he was probably right. But I also figured "everybody" couldn't include Gary the Gorilla. How could it? After all Gary had done? After all the preparations we'd made to get him? And let's not forget about my becoming the camp hero. Whatever else, let's not forget that.

At least that's what part of me was thinking. The other part was thinking that Dale's speech might have everything to do with Gary.

I figured I had two choices . . . either listen to Dale and worry if I was doing the right thing . . . or study my assignment sheet from Jimmy Jack and prepare to clobber Gary.

With a deep breath I pulled Jimmy Jack's paper out of my pocket and began to study.

I figure by now you're wondering what type of guy is writing this. I mean, don't I ever listen to the Bible and stuff? Actually, I do. A lot. I've been going to Sunday school like from first grade on. It's just that . . . I don't know . . . sometimes other things kinda get in the way and jumble stuff up.

And this was definitely one of those times. I mean, I had a chance to be the star of the entire camp. Me, Wally McDoogle, Superhero. With that kind of opportunity staring you in the face, it's pretty hard to remember the little details. You know, like obeying God and stuff.

I suppose when you get right down to it, that's probably the main reason I'm writing this. To let you know, so you don't go off and make the same mistake. Uh, better make that *mistakes*.

* * * * *

6:00 P.M. Dinner. The Babes had followed Jimmy Jack's instructions to the letter. While the rest of us were out trying to drown ourselves in the lake, the Babes had volunteered to help the cook with dinner. What a sweet, innocent offer, right?

Not exactly. . . .

By now everyone knew the only stuff you could count on being able to eat at camp (other than the half-frozen burritos) were the desserts. That's 'cause they were bought already made and frozen. You know, stuff like frozen pies, frozen cakes, that sort of thing. The reason was simple . . . there wasn't a whole lot of damage the cook could do taking them from the freezer to your plate.

Anyway, that's why desserts were the only thing Gary and his Goons stole from the other kids. It was like a ritual. If you were unlucky enough to pass Gary with your meal tray, you were unlucky enough to lose your dessert. Plain and simple.

Tonight's dessert was pumpkin pie.

"Oh, can we fix those pies up nice and pretty?" the Babes asked.

"How?" the cook said.

"With whipped cream," the Babes offered.

"Good idea," the cook replied. "Why don't you girls take care of that. You'll find the whipped cream in the refrigerator."

But the girls didn't need the whipped cream in the refrigerator. They had some of their own. And it wasn't exactly *whipped* cream. It was more like *shaving* cream . . . shaving cream purchased at the convenience store down the road.

Later at dinner, Gary and his Goons thought they were having a lucky day. For some reason a lot more campers than normal seemed to be passing their table. This, of course, meant that the Goons had a lot more desserts than normal. Not only that, but for some reason the cook's helpers had been incredibly generous with the topping. For some reason each pie was piled high with thick, rich, creamy topping.

The Goons didn't suspect a thing. Oh sure, the pies tasted a little weird. But, hey, they came from the Toxic Waste Site. What could you expect? It wasn't until Gary and the boys were on their fourth or fifth piece that they began to suspect something was up.

Gary was the first to notice. It seemed no one else in the cafeteria was eating their dessert. It also seemed there were a lot of sidelong glances and snickerings going on.

But Gary's suspicions weren't confirmed until Goon One started hiccupping. Then Goon Two started. Pretty soon Gary also joined the chorus.

It wasn't the hiccups that were the problem. It was the bubbles that followed each hiccup— bubbles that floated mysteriously out of their mouths. It was also the foam that started running out of the corners of those mouths.

The campers could no longer help themselves. Suddenly, everyone broke out laughing. Suddenly, Gary turned beet red. And suddenly, he shouted my name at the top of his lungs.

"McDOOGLE!!!"

But he didn't stick around to chat. He and his Goons were too busy racing out of the cafeteria. They were too busy looking for the nearest water fountain so they could rinse and spit, rinse and spit. Something they'd probably be doing the rest of the night.

Now that they were out of the room all eyes turned to me. And once again the applause started. I've got to admit it felt pretty neat. No, actually it felt terrific . . . wonderful. Everything except the part where I caught Dale looking at me. I can't explain it exactly. It wasn't like he was mad or anything. It was more like he was just disappointed. Real disappointed.

I swallowed hard and tried to smile. If he was disappointed over this, just wait till he saw what was next. Jimmy Jack's plans had only begun. The little knot in my stomach returned. Only now it wasn't so little. Now it seemed to be taking up a whole lot more space down there.

Chapter 5

Oops . . .

When we got back to our cabin after dinner, the place was trashed. No surprise there. Gary and his buddies had obviously swung by to say a little "thank-you."

That made the score one to one. One set of mouths filled with shaving cream, one trashed cabin. Of course, I hoped that would be the end. But I couldn't have been more wrong.

As soon as it got dark, we began:

JIMMY JACK'S SUPER PLAN TO GET
THE GOONS IN THE MORNING.

That night each group followed their instructions to the letter:

—Opera and I dug a deep hole in the path
that led to the woods.

—Wall Street used her phone to call information. She got the number of the General Store in town. But that was only the beginning. Tomorrow morning she'd make an even more important call.

—The Eggheads had three assignments:

- *Group 1* quietly collected all the garbage (especially the slimy, smelly stuff from the kitchen).
- *Group 2* rigged up a long plank at the edge of our hole.
- *Group 3* tied a rope around the top of a young pine tree and pulled it all the way down to the ground.

—The Babes' job was simple: Charm all the rich kids with feather pillows to donate them to the cause.

—And the Jocks? Well, the Jocks didn't have to wait for morning to see their plan work . . .

First they connected all the garden hoses from the Maintenance Shack. Next, they attached one end to the outside faucet, ran the other end over to Gary's cabin, and quietly slipped it through the big crack under the door. Then they put tape all along the crack. Finally, they turned on the water.

Gary was the first to wake up. He'd been dreaming about a beautiful stream with beautiful running water. For a second after he woke, he thought he still heard that running water. Lying on his stomach, he frowned. *How could it be? I'm inside the cabin. There's no running water here.*

Obviously, he was still dreaming. He had to be. How else could he see a shoe floating past his nose?

A shoe?

Followed by a suitcase.

A SUITCASE?

And then the other shoe.

"A FLOOD!" Gary shouted as he bolted up in bed. "WE'RE IN A FLOOD!"

Without stopping to think (or even wake up), the other two Goons leaped from their bunks and hit the flooded floor. Splashing and slipping, they fell face first into the icy water. This was followed by more splashing, slipping, and falling as they kept screaming, *"A flood! A flood! A flood!"*

By now the whole camp stood outside their cabin busting a gut with laughter as the Goons kept banging on their door screaming, *"Let us out, a flood, a flood, a flood!"*

Finally, the door flew open, and the water swooshed out of the cabin along with the three of them, coughing and cussing. It was truly a sight to behold.

"McDOOGLE!" Gary screamed as he staggered to his feet dripping wet and gasping for air. "I'LL GET YOU FOR THIS!" he shouted, searching the crowd. *"I'LL GET YOU!"*

But McDoogle was nowhere to be found. I'd already made a beeline back to my cabin where I'd be safe and sound. Or so I thought. . . .

* * * * *

The best I figure, it was about five the next morning when I woke up. There was a tickling feeling on my face. Even though I was half-asleep I knew it was just a joke. Opera or one of the guys was tickling me with a feather or something. It was an old trick to make me think something was crawling on me.

"Come on, guys," I mumbled.

But the tickling continued. Now I felt it over my arms and legs, too. Opera probably had the whole cabin helping in the joke.

"Give it up, Opera. Go back to bed."

But he didn't answer.

"Opera?"

Finally, I heard him mumble and mutter from his bunk above me. If you asked me, it was a pretty lousy imitation of someone pretending to be asleep.

"Opera, you're not fooling anyone."

The tickling grew worse. Finally, I pried my eyes open. "Okay, guys, the joke's ov—"

But there were no guys. There was no Opera. There was nobody. Just a zillion little black ants crawling all over me!

"AHHHHHH!" I screamed as I leaped out of my bed and began dancing around trying to slap them off.

"OOOOOOO! . . ." Opera cried as he tumbled down from his bed and began his own version of the dance.

Soon everyone in the cabin was jumping out of bed, shouting and dancing and slapping. "AHHHH, OOOOOO, OWWWWW, EEEEEE . . ."

The entire cabin had been crisscrossed with streams of honey. The sticky goo was everywhere. On the floor, on our beds, and all over our bodies. And wherever there was honey, there were ants . . . lots and lots of ants.

"AHHHH, OOOOOO, OWWWW, EEEEEE . . ."

"The showers!" I yelled. "Hit the showers!"

When we threw open our cabin door, you couldn't miss the thick trail of ants that swarmed underneath it. The thick trail of ants that followed a thick trail of honey. Honey that someone had laid from the anthills in the woods all the way to our cabin.

We finally arrived at the showers. *Nice work, Gary,* I thought as I stripped down and stepped into the icy cold water. *That makes the score two to two. Hope you're ready for the tie breaker. 'Cause it's coming up, and it's coming up real soon.*

* * * * *

8:57 A.M. and counting . . .

Everything was set. Everyone was ready. The ant attack was history. It was nothing compared to our plans for the greatest humiliation of all time.

8:58 A.M. and counting . . .

—The hole was dug and filled with the slimiest of garbage.
—Wall Street had phoned the General Store and convinced them to make an emergency delivery of chocolate syrup.
—The Babes had ripped the pillows and carefully placed them on the bent pine tree.
—Everyone was hiding along the path—everyone but me. I was the bait.

8:59 A.M. and counting . . .

We all knew that Gary and his Goons snuck into the woods for a smoke after breakfast. We all knew they had to come down this path to be at the softball field for Dale's 9:00 A.M. talk. We had everything calculated and planned to the exact minute.

So now I stood on the path, waiting. I wasn't thrilled about being the bait, but I was the logical choice. After all, I was the hero. I gave a nervous look at the hole in front of me. It was covered with a bed sheet and a thin layer of leaves to disguise it and make it look like the rest of the path.

9:00 A.M.!

Our digital watch/alarms went off like a flock of chirping birds.

And then, right on time . . . "Hey, Weasel!"

It was Gary!

He threw a sneer at his partners. They picked up their pace toward me. They couldn't believe their luck. There I was, their worst enemy, alone and defenseless. Or so they thought.

"Don't move," he growled. "I want to talk to you."

I swallowed hard and glanced at the hidden hole between us. "Sure," I squeaked.

I looked back at Gary and the Goons. Ten more steps and they'd be in the hole, swimming in the slimy garbage. But that was only the beginning. Yes sir, it was going to be wonderful.

Then something happened. Something we'd never planned. Something our worst imaginings never imagined.

"Hey, Wally?"

It was Dale! He was coming around the bend behind me!

"There you are. Listen, we've got to talk about last night."

Oh, please, God, anything but this!

I snapped my head back to Gary. Six more steps. Six more steps to go and he'd crash into the pit . . . right in front of Dale! I had to act fast. Quickly, I raced around the covered hole to Gary's side. "Hold it!" I shouted.

"Oh, Gary," Dale grinned, "you're here too, good."

Gary suddenly looked disappointed. He obviously figured Dale was coming to my rescue again. But not this time. This time no one could rescue me. Not when Dale was walking *directly toward us and the pit!*

"Dale, don't—!" I shouted and started toward him. But I didn't get far. Ol' Gorilla Boy grabbed me by the back of the shirt where Dale couldn't see.

"You're not getting away this time," he muttered.

"But you don't under—"

"No way."

"Hey look, guys," Dale said, coming closer and closer to the pit. "It's time you knock this stuff off."

"Look out," I tried to say, but Gary had my shirt pulled so tight that the words stuck in my throat.

"What do you mean?" Gary asked innocently.

"You know what I mean," Dale answered.

My eyes were as big as saucers. Forget saucers, how 'bout satellite dishes. Four more steps. Four more steps and Dale was a goner. I looked desperately toward my partners hiding in the bushes. They were nowhere to be seen.

"I'm talking about all these stunts you've been pulling," Dale said as he continued to approach. Three more steps . . . two more steps . . . one more step and . . .

I couldn't watch. I closed my eyes. But nothing happened.

Nothing at all.

I took a peek. Miraculously, Dale had come to a stop. He had reached the edge of the hole but went no further! I couldn't believe it! What luck!

"Stunts?" Gary asked, still playing it all innocent. "We're not pulling any stunts, are we Wease—er, Wally?" He let go of my shirt just long enough so I could answer.

"Stunts?" I coughed.

Dale looked me straight in the eyes. But I couldn't look back. I was too busy watching his feet. I was too busy watching them teeter on the edge of the pit. Just one inch forward and everything would give way. Just one inch forward and my career as a kid would be over.

"I don't mind some good-natured fun," Dale continued. He shoved his hands into his pockets and began rocking back and forth like he always did when he lectured. And with each rock he seemed to tip a little closer to the edge. "But there's nothing fun about what you guys are pulling. Not only is it mean, but it's downright dangerous. Hasn't anything I've said about wisdom gotten through to you guys?"

"YES!" I cried in a panic. *"EVERYTHING! EVERYTHING!"*

Dale looked at me, puzzled.

So did Gary.

"He gets kind of emotional," Gary offered.

After a second, Dale continued. "Look, all I'm suggesting is that . . ." And then it happened. He rocked forward just a little too far and suddenly dropped out of sight—right into the chest-deep pit of slimy garbage.

It was like a nightmare watching him wallow in it—slipping, sliding, falling, finally regaining his balance, and then beginning the routine all over again.

But that was only for starters. Pretty soon he spotted the board we had hung out over the hole.

"NO!" I cried out. "Not the board!" But no one heard.

I watched in horror as Dale grabbed hold of the board for help. But it was another one of our traps. For as the board tipped toward him, so did a huge drum of chocolate syrup at the other end. A huge drum of chocolate syrup that tipped over and spilled out all of its contents.

WHOOSH . . . GLUG-GLUG-GLUG . . .

The chocolate syrup washed over Dale like a flood. Suddenly, he no longer looked like a counselor. Suddenly, he looked very much like a giant, chocolate-covered peanut.

He came up out of the flood coughing and sputtering. Unfortunately, it wasn't over yet . . . not quite.

When the drum emptied, it triggered the rope that tied down the nearby pine tree. The pine tree snapped up, sending the contents of eight feather pillows high into the air . . . directly over the pit.

As the feathers gently floated down into the hole, they began to stick all over Dale's gooey body. No longer did our counselor look like a giant, chocolate-covered peanut. Now he looked like a giant, chocolate-covered chicken.

Gary looked at me. I looked at Gary.

"Oops" was all I could think of to say.

Chapter 6

Uh-Oh . . .

Dale's 9:00 A.M. talk on wisdom didn't exactly start at 9:00 A.M. He had a little cleaning up to do. Actually, he had a lot of cleaning up to do. There's something about the way dried chocolate syrup and chicken feathers stick in the hair that makes them a little tricky to wash out.

We all sat on the bleachers, silently waiting—like prisoners for execution. Even Jimmy Jack wasn't saying much—an all-time first for him.

I glanced over at Gary. Our eyes met. He slowly shook his head in amazement. I wanted to explain. I wanted to tell him that it really wasn't my fault . . . that it was all Jimmy Jack's idea . . . that all the other kids in camp helped. But it wouldn't have made any difference.

There was no telling when Dale would show up, but none of us complained about sitting around. We would have sat there all day if we had to. So to pass away the time, I reached down to Ol' Betsy, popped open her lid, and snapped her on.

Maybe a little Mutant Man would help . . .

As you may recall, our incredibly handsome hero is orbiting the planet Jupiter. It's a beautiful view up there. Not a cloud in the sky. Come to think of it, there isn't a sky. Come to think about it, there isn't even any air. And since Mutant Man has this thing about breathing, he figures it's best to be moving along...fast!

But how?

Suddenly, he spots a stray meteor blazing past. What luck! Normally, superheros don't hitchhike. I mean, these days there's no telling what type of weirdos might be hanging around the block—or the outer fringes of the galaxy for that matter.

But Mutant Man has no choice. Dr. Ghastly is still back on earth sucking up wisdom. Who knows what humongous havoc he's havocking while our hero's hidden away. And let's not forget that *Brady Bunch* rerun. If the mighty Mutant doesn't hurry back, he'll miss the entire show!

Pressing the button on his Muton-Belt, the left hand of our gorgeous good guy suddenly turns into a giant catcher's mitt.

"Okay, Buddy Boy," he shouts in his best Major League catcher's voice. "Burn her right in here, attaboy, what say, what say, come on, burn it in, burn it in."

And "burn in" is exactly what the meteor does.

K-SWOOSH-SIZZLE-SIZZLE-SIZZLE.

Immediately, Mutant's mitt is on fire. Talk about too hot to handle. Fortunately, our handy hunk carries a fire extinguisher in his back pocket for just such occasions.

Soon the fire is out as the meteor hurtles our hero toward the earth at a zillion-point-three miles per hour.

Next he presses the radar button on his belt, which not only spots Dr. Ghastly's helicopter, but also heats up last night's leftovers for a little between-adventures snack.

Finally, he makes his move. "Thanks for the lift!" he shouts as he lets go of the fiery meteor and falls toward earth. Normally, such a fantastic free fall would frighten even our fearless and faithful friend (say that five times fast). But as an owner of several skateboards, Mutant is a pro at falling.

At last Dr. Ghastly comes into view. His Wisdom Sucker Upper is still doing some serious sucking. But...OH NO! COULD IT BE? Our hero is falling too fast. According to his rough-but-always-brilliant calculations, he'll be missing the Gorilla by 17 yards, 2 feet, and $2\frac{1}{2}$ inches (give or take a mile). Great Scott! What can he do?

No need to worry your pretty little head. Superheros are always prepared for such emergencies. Reaching into his other back pocket, he pulls out a piece of Muton Sugarless Bubblegum— the preferred gum of superheros every- where. Quickly popping it into his mouth, he chews and blows a bubble. But not just any bubble. This is a

Muton Bubble—so big that it could pass for a hot air balloon!

And, amazingly enough, that's exactly what it becomes!

Expertly, he maneuvers the balloon toward Dr. Ghastly. Once beside the hairy ape's helicopter, he pops the bubble and makes a superb superhero leap toward the cockpit. It's a close call, but he makes it. He has to. There are still five more chapters left in this book.

Now inside, they begin a fearsome fight. Holding each other in their clutches, they dance this way and that. That way and this. Pretty soon they're doing the fox trot, then the hokey-pokey, then...

But hold the phone! This is no time for dance class!

In one swift move, Mutant reaches over, turns off the helicopter's key, and throws it out the window. The chopper chugs to a stop. A brilliant move. Now the helicopter will glide safely to earth, and they can finish their fight on the ground. There's only one little detail...this

helicopter doesn't glide. It falls.
Like a rock.

Ahhhh! Dr. Ghastly screams.

Ohhhh! Mutant Man cries.

The ground races at them.

"What do we do!?" yells Ghastly.

"You're the supervillain," Mutant
shouts. "Think of something!"

"Yeah, but this is your story!"

Whatever they do, they'll have to
do it together. And whatever they do,
they'll have to do it quickly.
Because in just 5.8 seconds they'll
be hitting the earth. Better make
that 4.7 seconds...Ah, 3.6...2.5...
Come on, guys...1.4...

"Shhh! Here he is; here he comes now." The
crowd grew quiet as Dale approached the
bleachers. I quickly shut down Ol' Betsy and
waited.

The guy looked pretty good—except for the
chocolate syrup still around his fingernails and
the faint aroma of rotting garbage.

"Well," he said slowly, looking around the
group. And by looking I don't mean a quick
glance. I mean, this guy managed to lock eyes

with every one of us. "To say I'm disappointed might be an understatement. Deeply discouraged is more like it . . ."

I squirmed in my seat. This was going to be worse than I thought. Why didn't the guy just scream at us like all the other grownups?

"I don't know what more I can do. Haven't our talks on wisdom meant anything?"

We all stared at the bleacher seats in front of us . . . hard, real hard.

Dale continued. "We've discussed how it's wise to choose good friends."

I threw a look over at Opera and Wall Street. They were good friends. Then I spotted Jimmy Jack. Well, two out of three ain't bad.

"We've talked about the wisdom of being kind to others."

I threw a look over at Gary and his Goons. Strike Two.

"And we've said that wisdom is more than just learning what God wants. It's *doing* what He wants. Wisdom is obeying."

Strike Three.

"I actually thought you guys were listening. That is, until last night. . . ." He reached into his ear and pulled out a small feather. "And this morning."

More silence.

"I don't know," he sighed. "I'm almost tempted to cancel today's canoe trip."

The canoe trip? With all of the excitement, I'd completely forgotten about the canoe trip!

But the rest of the campers hadn't. A murmur of protest swept through the crowd until Dale raised his hands. "But I don't think so."

The murmurs turned to sighs of relief.

"That's too easy."

The sighs stopped. What could be worse than canceling the canoe trip? We were about to find out. Forget being tortured on the rack, forget the electric chairs, forget a day without TV. What Dale had planned for us was worse than all those punishments put together.

"You know," he continued calmly, "the Bible tells us that it's also wise to settle conflicts peacefully. And if I'm not mistaken, we definitely have some conflict going here. Wouldn't you say so, Gary? Wally?"

Every eye in the camp turned to Gary and me. Yes sir. Dale was definitely up to something.

"So . . . to help you better understand wisdom I've devised a little competition of my own. Starting at noon, Gary and Wally will begin a competition that will teach you wisdom in a way that you will never forget."

The group started to buzz. But Dale was on

a roll. "Over and over again the Bible talks
about the wisdom of serving others and of lov-
ing your enemy. So . . ."

Uh-oh, I thought, *here it comes.*

"For the next two days—throughout our
entire canoe trip—Wally and Gary will be competing . . . competing to see which of them can
*out*serve and *out*love the other."

The group buzzed louder.

"If Gary wins, Wally's group will have to pick
up all the trash around camp before we go home.
If Wally wins, that will be Gary's group's job."

The buzzing turned to a loud drone. Was the
guy crazy? Who ever heard of this kind of pun-
ishment—having to outserve the other guy?

"Wall Street," he called, "you will be the
score- keeper for Wally. Jimmy Jack, you keep
track of Gary's score."

Jimmy Jack started to protest, but Dale cut
him off. "Now, we all have some serious packing
to do for the trip, so I suggest we get started."
Then, without another word, he turned and
headed back toward the cabins.

The loud drone of the group turned to a roar.
But I barely noticed. My head was too busy
spinning. I mean, let's face it, on the McDoogle
scale of craziness, this was definitely pushing
an 11. But things were going to get even crazier.

Chapter 7

The Competition Begins

"The guy's nuts!" Opera shouted. "Loony Tunes." He threw another handful of cassettes into his backpack on the bed. "Whoever heard of a competition where you have to outserve the other guy?"

I nodded in silent agreement.

"If you ask me—"

But no one had time to ask. Suddenly, there was a loud knock at the door. More like a bunch of mini-explosions.

Opera and I both went cold.

"Who is it?" I asked.

More banging. "Open up, Weasel, it's me!"

I swallowed hard. There was no mistaking Gary the Gorilla's cheery voice.

"What do you want?" Opera shouted.

"I've come. . . ." For a moment it sounded like he couldn't quite squeeze out the words. He tried again. "I've come to . . . help you . . . pack."

Opera threw me a look. "It's a trap!" he whispered. "Don't fall for it."

The next voice belonged to Jimmy Jack. It was as smooth and slippery as ever. "Come on, Wally, he's telling the truth."

I hesitated a moment.

"Don't do it man, it's a trap!" Opera repeated. He yanked what was left of his Walkman off his head and stuffed it out of sight.

I reached for the door, took a deep breath and opened it . . . I barely got it cracked before Gary yanked it out of my hands and threw it open. "Here," he growled, "allow me."

"All right!" Jimmy Jack cried. He put a mark in the notebook he was carrying. "That's one good-deed point for Gary."

I stood stunned. It was amazing how quickly Jimmy Jack had changed sides. But, hey, we are talking about Jimmy Jack Hucksterly, here.

"You packed yet?" the Gorilla demanded as he shoved his way past me.

"Well, yeah, almost."

He began rifling through my backpack. "What about socks? I don't see no socks."

"I was just about—"

"Here. . . ." He spotted my open drawer full of socks. In one quick move he yanked it out and dumped the entire contents into my backpack. "Have some socks," he said with a laugh.

"Gary scores again!" Jimmy Jack shouted. "That's two points for Gary, zero points for—"

"Not so fast." We looked back toward the door and saw Wall Street. She stood there holding her own notebook and a calculator. "The idea is to serve in kindness and love," she continued. "And since Gary's present attitude is more harmful than helpful, I'm deducting ⅜ of a point from his score." She began working her calculator. "Let's see, ⅜ of a point from a previous score of 1 brings your current score to a total of ⅝ of a point."

We just stood and stared. No doubt about it, Wall Street was definitely going to be a stockbroker. Then, without a word, Gary reached for my socks and started putting some back in the drawer. Neatly . . . very, very neatly.

* * * * *

By the time we got to the dock with our canoe, Gary's stock, . . . er, score was up to 25 and ⅞. Mine was a mere 23 and ¾. He'd gotten the jump on me with the packing and stuff, but I was hot on his trail. Already I'd:

—cleaned out the tread of his hightops,
—put toothpaste on his toothbrush,
—and cleaned the whiskers out of his sink.

(Imagine a sixth grader with whiskers. I guess that's why they call him the Gorilla.)

Now we were at the dock with the rest of the camp trying to put our canoe in the water. I held one end, Gary held the other. I guess Dale figured by putting us together we might become friends.

Guess again. For starters we couldn't even agree which side of the dock to put the canoe in.

"This side," Gary barked, "put it over here."

"But Gary," I complained, hanging on to my end. "There's more room on this side."

"But Gary, it's easier if we—"

"Let go!"

"Ga—"

"LET ME HAVE IT!" He lifted the entire canoe and spun my end out over the water. It was an impressive move. The only problem was I was still hanging on!

"Gary!" I shouted as I hung out over the water clinging to the canoe for my life. "Gary, put me back!"

The first thing I saw in his face was surprise. Then anger. And finally . . . revenge. And why not? After all, here was his chance. A chance to get even, and make a fool out of me, all at the same time. It was the perfect opportunity.

But the thought only lasted a second. Because

in that second he spotted Wall Street out of the corner of his eye. Calculator in hand, she stood anxiously waiting to make another deduction on his score.

Immediately, he changed his mind. Just as quickly as he had spun me out, Gary struggled to bring me in. But this time things didn't go quite so smoothly.

"Gary!" I shouted as he started to stagger under the weight. "Gary!"

Kids ducked out of the way. Some dropped their canoes, others ran for their lives as Gary lumbered this way, then that.

"Gary, don't drop me!"

At last he spun me over to the dock so I could let loose. But when I let go, the sudden weight loss threw him off balance. He stumbled to the left two steps and then to the right four. Unfortunately, he only had room for three. The fourth step sent him crashing into the water.

He came to the surface sputtering and coughing. Of course, he was totally soaked and totally steamed. And, of course, everyone was laughing their heads off.

Everyone but me. I can't explain it exactly, but I almost felt sorry for the guy. *Almost.* I mean, here he was trying to help me, to do me a favor, and look what happened.

I dropped to my knees and offered him my hand. "Here," I said.

He looked at me with suspicion before finally reaching out. Unfortunately, Wall Street was right beside me writing in her notebook. "Good work, Wally. You get 1 and ½ points for helping."

Without a word Gary let go of my hand. Of course, he went splashing back into the water and, of course, there was more laughter.

So much for making friends.

* * * * *

Two hours later, Gary and I had paddled about two feet. Everyone else had followed Dale down to the end of the lake where the river started. Everyone else was sitting along the shore resting and eating lunch. Everyone but us.

We were too busy going in tight little circles, around and around to the right. And then when we got tired of that, we started going around and around to the left. I was in the front. Gary was in the back.

"Will you stop paddling so hard?" I complained.

"Paddle harder," he ordered.

"Paddle to the left."

"The right."

"Will you please stop paddling?"

"Can't you keep up?"

"You're steering us sideways!"

"Can't you do anything?"

"Shut up!"

"You shut up!"

And so it went. We worked harder and did more paddling than the whole camp combined. But you wouldn't know it. And minute by minute, hour by hour, the phrase *"getting nowhere fast"* took on a whole new meaning.

Bushed and beat (not to mention starved), we finally caught up with the others and started toward shore. But the others were already pushing off.

"Where you guys going?" Dale asked as he pulled his canoe beside ours.

"What's it look like?" Gary growled. "To the shore."

"I don't think so. Lunch break's over."

"What?" I gasped.

"You've already put us an hour behind. Let's get going."

"We got to eat something, man. We got to catch our breath."

"Sorry guys, what you've got to do is push out."

"Dale . . ."

"Maybe if you worked together, this sort of thing wouldn't happen. Anyway, it's time to go."

Without another word he gave the nose of our canoe a push. Before we knew it, we were headed back out into the water.

I was mad. Not only at Gary, but also at Dale. It wasn't my fault I had such a loser for a partner. Of course, if you asked Gary, he was probably thinking the same thing about me. I guess, in a sense, we were both right. Little did we know we'd both have to change our thinking. Soon. Very, very soon.

Chapter 8

Revelations

Once we started going downriver it was a little easier to stay with the group (even though we zig-zagged all over the place).

As the hours dragged, Gary and I grew hungrier and hungrier. But even that didn't stop us from trying to rack up points on each other.

"Hey, Jimmy Jack!" Gary called to the canoe up ahead. "How many points I get for giving the Weasel here my granola bar?"

"Under the circumstances . . . ten points!" Jimmy Jack shouted.

"No way!" Wall Street called from two canoes over. "Two and ⅜ max."

"Eight and ⅝," Jimmy Jack argued.

"Five and ¼ and we got a deal."

"Sold!" Jimmy Jack shouted as they both went for their notebooks and jotted down the number.

Gary handed the bar up to me, and I took a bite. It was perfect. Just what I needed. But I was no fool. "Wall Street," I called. "How many points I get if I give half of it back to him?"

"Seven even," she offered.

"Two and ½," Jimmy Jack countered.

"Five and it's a deal."

Again they went for their notebooks.

I turned back to Gary and started to hand him the granola bar. And then it happened. . . .

THUD!

We hit a huge boulder sticking out of the river. Before I could push away with my paddle the current caught the back of the canoe and started turning us around.

"To the left!" I yelled. "Paddle to the left!"

But it did no good. Before we knew it we were going down the river sideways.

"To the left," I kept shouting. "To the left!" But whatever Gary was doing, he wasn't paddling us to the left. He was paddling us straight toward another boulder.

"WATCH IT!" I screamed.

SCRAPE-SCREECH . . .

The canoe came to a stop on a large flat rock. We were grounded. But for only a second. The current pushed and tugged until the whole canoe started to tip.

"HANG ON!"

"TO THE LEFT! PUSH TO THE LEFT!"

"YOU'RE ROCKING US. . . . STOP ROCK-ING THE—"

"GARY, PUSH TO THE—"

"LOOK OUT!"

And just like that, we were in the water . . . the *freezing* water. But it wasn't the cold that we were worried about.

"Grab the paddles!" I shouted. "Don't let the paddles get away!"

We dove after them.

"My sleeping bag," Gary shouted. "Get my sleeping bag!"

I made a lunge for it but missed. The current had already picked it up and swept it into the main channel of the river. We watched help-lessly as it disappeared out of sight.

"Oh man," Gary groaned. "My brother's going to kill me." (Of course, he had a few other choice words to say, but since I'm supposed to be a Chris-tian and stuff I don't think I can write them.)

Ten minutes later we were back in our canoe shivering up a storm. I talked Gary into letting me sit in the back so I could steer. It cost 3 and ⅛ points, but it was a small price to pay to keep us going in the right direction. I knew there was something weird about the way Gary steered and paddled. I didn't know how weird until he sat in front of me.

"Gary, don't you know how to paddle?"

"Of course I do, what do you take me for?" He grabbed his paddle tighter and shoved it back into the water all crooked and cockeyed like.

Suddenly, all our zigzagging made sense. Don't get me wrong, I'm no canoe expert, but Gary didn't know beans about paddling. I can't explain it, but he held it in his hands all backward and twisted.

"A baseball bat," I said, "you hold it like a baseball bat."

"Oh, right, a baseball bat, sure." He fumbled with the paddle a little but wound up holding it even worse than before.

"Gary . . ."

"What now?"

"A baseball bat," I repeated. "You've held a baseball bat before."

"Maybe I have and maybe I haven't."

"You've never held a baseball bat?" I couldn't hide the amazement in my voice. What type of kid never held a baseball bat? "Didn't your dad ever show you how to hold a baseball bat?"

"Yeah," he snorted in contempt, "like I'm sure my old man's going to play baseball with me."

I started to answer but let it go. It was like a new Gary began to appear in front of me. As I kept watching him struggle and fight with the simple little job of paddling, I started—I don't know—I started to feel kind of sorry for him. Sure I could have laughed and made all sorts of jokes. But somehow it wasn't funny. Instead, it was kind of sad. I mean, if no one showed him simple stuff like holding a baseball bat, what else didn't they show him?

Who knew what this guy's life was really like. Who knew what type of stuff he had to put up with at home. Maybe, underneath that tough exterior there was a tender, sensitive heart that just needed—

"Listen, Moron," he snarled at me from over his shoulder. "If you don't start paddling, I'll bash your brains in."

I started paddling with all of my might . . . but I also kept watching.

* * * * *

A few hours later we set up camp with everyone else. Opera and my group cheered me on while Gary's Goons did the same for him. We were both scoring points like crazy. You see, we'd each figured out that if we let the other guy help us and score some points off us, then we were actually helping him, which meant we should be scoring even more points for ourself!

Confusing? You bet. Especially when the conversations went like this:

"Here, Gary, I brought over your dinner."
> *(I score 5 and ½ points.)*

"I didn't want you to get my dinner."
> *(I lose 5 and ½ points.)*

"Please, go ahead and take it."
> *(I score 5 and ½ points.)*

"Well, all right," Gary sighs. "But only if it will help you score."
> *(Gary scores 10 points.)*

See what I mean about confusing? And we went around and around like that all night. Everything from getting refills on hot chocolate, to untying each other's shoes, to slapping off the other guy's mosquitoes. Talk about exhausting. But the last one, the one when we got ready for bed, that's the one I'll never forget. . . .

"You're still in your wet clothes." I said. "You can't sleep in them, let me get you some dry ones."

"Don't bother."

"No bother," I said as I got up and walked over to his duffel bag."

"I don't need any—"

"Sure you do," I said, picking up the bag.

"McDoogle!"

But he was too late. I already had the thing unzipped. Inside there was nothing but a couple pairs of used socks (very used), a worn T-shirt or two, and some cut-offs. "Where's the rest of your clothes?" I asked. "Didn't you bring them?"

"Of course I brought 'em," he sneered. "I just, uh, they're . . ." he faltered for a second. "They were in with my sleeping bag. Yeah, they were rolled up inside the sleeping bag that you let float off."

"Oh," I said, not buying a word of it. "Well, you can't sleep in wet clothes."

"They're fine," he shrugged.

"Listen, my mom packed an extra blanket (along with an extra everything else in the world). Why don't you use it?"

"I don't need your stupid blanket," he growled.

I was stumped. The guy was obviously lying, and he obviously needed a blanket. What could I do? Then a thought came to mind. A pretty good one. "Listen, Gary, I'm a bit behind in the points. You'd be doing me a real favor if you let me score by loaning you this blanket."

He looked at me a long moment.

"Come on, just this once. I'll owe you."

"Well, all right," he finally muttered, "but just this once."

"Thanks." I grinned. At least I was grinning

on the outside. On the inside, I was really starting to hurt for the guy. I mean, he didn't have
anybody to teach him sports stuff. He didn't
have anybody to pack him decent clothes. What
else didn't he have?

Later, as everyone lay in bed, I thought I'd
find out. "Gary?" I asked.

"Now what?" he mumbled.

"I was wondering. Why did you, like, you
know, come here?"

"What?"

"To church camp. I mean, you don't go to
church or Sunday school or anything like that,
do you?"

There was a long pause. Finally, he answered.
"Dale paid my way."

"Dale?!" I couldn't hide the surprise in my
voice.

"Yeah, he swings by every once in a while to
see how me and Mom are doing."

"Oh," I said, trying to sound matter of fact.
But my mind began to race. So Dale already
knew this guy. So Dale saw something in him,
too. So Dale was actually trying to help. Hmm . . .

An hour later Gary and the rest of the camp
were sound asleep. But my mind still hadn't
shut down. Since there was no way to find the
"off" switch and since I was still thinking about

Gary, I finally sat up and took a good look at him. There he was, curled into a little ball under my one thin blanket. It was funny, but asleep like that he didn't look so tough or so mean. In fact, he looked kind of . . . helpless. He also looked cold. Real cold.

I crawled out of my sleeping bag and immediately found out why he looked so cold. It *was* cold. It was freezing. I reached over to my backpack and quickly slipped on a coat and a pair of long johns Mom had packed. (Packing thermal underwear in the middle of summer may seem strange, but then again, you don't know Mom.)

Next I unzipped my sleeping bag all the way around to make it flat like a blanket. Finally, I got to my feet and carried the flattened bag over to Gary. I looked down at him a moment. He seemed even smaller and more helpless than before. Gently, I laid the bag across him. He stirred a little but didn't wake up. Good.

I glanced over to where Wall Street was sleeping. For a second, I thought of waking her up and scoring about a zillion points—you know, for being such a good deed doer. But somehow . . . I don't know. I guess somehow I knew this deed should be on the house.

Imagine my surprise when I turned and saw Dale standing beside me. In his hand was an extra sleeping bag. "I thought you might need this," he said, handing it to me. Then, before I could answer, he turned and headed back to his tent. Talk about amazement. I tell you, the guy never seemed to run out of surprises.

Chapter 9
Danger ... Big Time

The next morning Gary didn't say a word about the sleeping bag. When I came back from brushing my teeth, it was rolled up and stuffed into my backpack like nothing had ever happened. But something *had* happened. Something had happened to me, and maybe, just maybe, something had started to happen to Gary.

I noticed it when we began forgetting about points. I noticed it when we didn't fire off quite so many put-downs. And I noticed it the most when Dale gave his last talk on wisdom.

The canoes were loaded and everyone was ready to push off, so Dale made it short and sweet. "I hope over this last week you've all seen the importance of wisdom."

The group nodded. Some of us more than others.

"But no study on wisdom would be complete

without mentioning the greatest wisdom of all
. . . the wisdom of asking Jesus Christ to forgive
you of all your wrongs . . . the wisdom of asking
Him to come inside to be the Lord of your life."

I threw a glance at Gary. He was staring at
Dale real hard—but not like he wanted to flatten
him. This time it was more like he was listening.

Now me, I'd heard it all a million times
before—how Jesus died on the cross for our sins
and how we need to let Him control our life and
all that stuff. But ol' Gary, I tell you, the guy just
kept on staring and listening like he'd never
heard it before.

"Now, it can be a scary thing," Dale continued, "letting go of your life—letting go and completely trusting somebody else with it. But that's
what faith is all about. And the neat thing about
having faith in God is that He will never let you
down. No matter what you do, He'll never drop
you; He'll never let you go. You have my word on
it. Better yet, you have His. So, before we wrap
up, I just want to know if there's anyone here
who hasn't given God control of their life yet and
wants to."

I stole another glance over at Gary. He wasn't
looking at Dale anymore. Now he just sort of
stared at the ground . . . hard, real hard.

"Anyone at all?" Dale kept waiting. Gary

kept staring. It was almost like a private thing between them. Like Dale had made the speech just for Gary, and now he was waiting for him to make the decision.

But Gary didn't move. Not a muscle. He wasn't doing it out of stubbornness, though. By now I knew that much about him. Gary wasn't being stubborn, he was just being scared. Stop and think about it a second. I mean, the guy obviously didn't have any decent parents. He obviously didn't have any decent clothing. He probably didn't have any decent anything. All Gary had was himself. And if he gave that away, well . . . what was left?

I wanted to tell him I understood. I also wanted to lean over and tell him not to worry, that being a Christian was pretty cool. But I knew I hadn't been the best example. So I just sort of stood beside him and kept my mouth shut.

Finally, Dale closed with a little prayer. Then he gave us some last-minute instructions. About three miles downstream there would be a parking lot to the right. We were supposed to dock our canoes there, load them on the trailer rack, and hop on the bus back to camp. He warned us not to paddle past the parking lot. "There's some really heavy white water just downstream. I don't want any of you hotshots goofing off and getting near it. Got it?"

We got it. Before he could think of anything else to say, we shoved our canoes into the water and took off.

For the longest time, Gary and I didn't say a word. I just steered from the back trying to straighten our zigzags as Gary sat in the front doing a worse imitation of paddling than he did the day before.

But the silence couldn't last long. I knew I had to say something. I'd never talked to anybody about God before (though I know we're supposed to). And I wasn't too keen on starting off with somebody like Gary. But after last night and after Dale's little talk, well, I had to say something . . . anything. So, after pushing my glasses back on my face and muttering a little prayer for help, I started:

"That Dale, he's something."

No answer.

"Gary?"

"I heard you."

I tried again. "He's a pretty cool guy, huh?"

"He's all right."

I swallowed, took another breath, and tried a third time. "I mean, you can really trust him and stuff."

No answer.

"Especially what he says about God. You

know, about letting go and trusting Him and everything. Sure, it's kind of scary, but you know, the thing is—"

"Weasel?"

"Yeah, Gary."

"Shut up."

Well, that about wrapped up my days as an evangelist. Billy Graham could rest easy. No way I'd be taking over his job. Or so I thought. But in less than an hour things started to pop.

"There it is," I called. "There's the parking lot."

Everyone was turning in and pushing toward shore. Well, almost everyone. "To the right," I called. "Start paddling to the right."

"I got it," Gary said.

But he didn't have it. In fact, the more he paddled, the further he pushed us to the left, the further he pushed us *away* from shore.

"Gary, I know what I'm talking about. To the right."

"Shut up, I've got it."

By now we were drawing the attention of everyone back at shore. "Hey, Wally!" Opera shouted. "Where you going?"

I didn't answer. I had a few other things on my mind. "Will you just let me paddle?" I snapped, not quite so politely.

"I said shut up!" Gary shouted even less politely.

"If you're not going to do it right, let me do it!"

But nothing I said worked. That shouldn't have been a big surprise. After all, everyone was standing on the shore gawking. And everyone knows the number one rule in the Bully's Handbook is "Never, *never* let some four-eyed wimp outdo you—especially in public." So Gary kept right on paddling . . . even if it was in the wrong direction.

"Wally . . . Gary . . ." The voices from shore grew fainter as we kept on paddling—each of us fighting for control, neither of us giving an inch.

And then I heard it. It was a muffled kind of roar. But a muffled roar that got louder by the second.

"It's the rapids!" I shouted. "We've got to get to shore!"

"I'm trying!" Gary yelled. "I'm trying!"

We paddled as hard as we could, any way that we could. But nothing worked. Every second the current got faster. And every second our chances of getting out got smaller.

"Paddle on the left!" I shouted. But it did no good.

The roar was much louder. And for good reason. We were now, officially, in the rapids!

The first set wasn't so bad. *Scrape-splash! Scrape-splash.* We shot over the tops of the rocks and dipped hard into the water—again and again. It was almost fun. *Almost.* But not quite. And not for long.

"We got to get out of here!" Gary shouted from the front. "There's bigger ones ahead!" He paddled even harder, which put us in even worse shape until . . .

Thump-Crash! Thump-Crash! We shot over our first rocks.

"Do something!" Gary shouted over the roar and the spray.

"I'm doing, I'm doing!" I shouted as I tried to paddle.

"LOOK OUT!" Gary cried as we shot over another group of boulders. *Thump-Crash! Thump-Crash! Thump-Crash!*

I tried to push off the passing rocks with the paddle. But we were going too fast. *Thump-Crash! Thump-Crash!* It was like a roller coaster out of control—only without seat belts!

"HANG ON!" Gary shouted. "HERE'S A BIG ONE!"

The canoe scraped against something, and for a second we slowed. Then suddenly we dipped forward and dropped straight down into a huge hole.

KERRR-SPLAAAASH! Water was everywhere. "GARY!" I coughed and sputtered. "GARY, WHERE ARE YOU?!"

"HERE!" he shouted as the water cleared and he came into view. He'd pitched his paddle and was hanging on to the edge of the canoe for dear life. "HANG ON!" he screamed. Again we fell. *KERRR-SPLAAAASH-CRINKLE-CRINKLE!* This time we weren't so lucky. That "CRINKLE-CRINKLE" was our canoe twisting in the middle. Quickly, it began filling up with water.

"JUMP!" I screamed. "JUMP!"

"YOU'RE CRAZY!"

"WE'VE GOT LIFE JACKETS—THE CANOE'S HISTORY. JUMP!"

Gary would have argued but something else caught his attention.

"A WATERFALL!" he cried.

Don't get me wrong, it wasn't Niagara Falls or anything like that. But for us it was big enough. We were still in the canoe when we shot over the edge and hung in midair for hours (or at least half a second). Then the front end dipped, and we found ourselves doing a nose-dive straight down.

"WE'RE GOING TO DIE!" we both shouted. (Which was the first thing we'd agreed upon during the whole trip.)

We hit the water hard and were thrown out of the canoe (or what was left of it). I was underwater now, I knew that. It was like a nightmare. Bubbles and water were everywhere. I was twirled and spun around so hard I couldn't tell which way was up. I knew I had to get to the surface. I just didn't know where the surface was. I crashed into the rocks again and again but didn't feel any pain. The only pain was in my lungs. They were about to explode. I had to get a breath. Water or no water, I needed to suck something into them. Then somewhere in the back of my mind I began to realize what was happening . . .

I'm drowning.

But instead of seeing my whole life pass before my eyes, all I could think of was, *Great, I'm probably the only one in the world who has drowned while wearing a life jacket. Now doesn't that just figure.*

When I couldn't hold off anymore, when I had to breathe or die, I suddenly bobbed to the surface—just like that.

I gulped in as much air as I could before I was dragged under again. But I was only under a second before I came back up coughing and choking. My glasses were gone, and I couldn't see a thing. But as far as I could tell it didn't much matter. Everything around me was roaring water.

"GARY!" I shouted. I don't know why I was suddenly worried about him. I had other details to worry about, you know, like saving my own life. But right then, he was all I could think of. "GARY!"

Then, almost beside me, he popped up, coughing and gagging. "WALLY?" he shouted, desperately looking for me. "WALLY!"

"I'M RIGHT HERE!"

He spun around. "I THOUGHT YOU DROWNED."

"NOT YET!"

"LOOK OUT!" he shouted.

I took a deep gulp of air and just in time. We both flew over another mini-waterfall and crashed into the water. More tumbling and spinning, but it wasn't quite as bad this time. (Either that or we were getting the hang of it.) Soon we were both at the surface coughing and gasping for air.

"WE GOT TO GRAB HOLD OF SOME-THING!" Gary shouted.

"WHAT?"

"THERE, OVER THERE!"

"I CAN'T SEE A THING!"

"GRAB HOLD OF ME!" Gary shouted.

"BUT I CAN'T SEE A—"

"SHUT UP AND GRAB HOLD OF ME!"

I obeyed. In a few seconds, we were at a huge tree limb that had wedged itself into the rocks.

"HANG ON TO THIS BRANCH!" he shouted. "HANG ON!"

He didn't have to tell me twice.

So there we were, both hanging onto a tree limb in the middle of a roaring river. Boy, if ever I could have used a hand from ol' Mutant Man, it would have been then. Of course, I didn't exactly have my computer handy. And I didn't exactly figure it would be much help . . . especially when the tree limb began to shudder under our weight . . . especially when it gave a slight groan and started to loosen.

Chapter 10

A Test of Faith

"WALLY . . . GARY!"

"It's Dale!" Gary shouted. I had to take his word for it. Without my glasses, all I saw was a dark, blurry blob (which must have been Dale) standing on a flat blurry blob (which must have been the shore).

"HANG ON!" Dale shouted.

What do you think we're going to do? I thought. *Go out for pizza?* But Gary shouted something a little more helpful. "HURRY! THE BRANCH IS GIVING WAY."

Almost like an answer, the branch gave another little groan, this time followed by a little *crack*.

"How you doing, Weasel?" Gary shouted.

"Pretty good!" I yelled. "What's going on?"

"They're tying a rope around Dale's waist."

A moment later I heard a splash and saw a

103

blurry form half wading, half swimming toward us.

The branch was full of a lot of sharp spines and stubby things. They cut into my hand pretty hard so I tried to grab the branch differently. It gave another little jerk followed by a louder *CRACK*.

"DON'T MOVE!" Gary shouted. "STOP MOVING!"

I looked back toward Dale. He was downstream from us about fifteen feet.

The branch quit cracking. Now it started creaking.

"OKAY, GUYS," Dale shouted. "ONE OF YOU LET GO FIRST."

"YOU'RE CRAZY!" Gary shouted. "NO WAY ARE WE LETTING GO! COME AND GET US!"

"I CAN'T! YOU'RE GOING TO HAVE TO LET GO AND LET ME CATCH YOU."

"WHAT?"

"LET GO AND THE CURRENT WILL CARRY YOU RIGHT TO ME!"

"NO WAY!"

"GARY, YOU GOT TO TRUST ME ON THIS. I WON'T LET YOU GO!"

"YOU'RE CRAZY!" he repeated.

The branch gave another little shudder and slipped some more.

"TRUST ME! GUYS, YOU GOT TO HAVE FAITH! HAVE FAITH THAT I WON'T LET YOU GO!"

"What's he doing," Gary smirked, "giving us another one of his speeches?"

I tried to smile back. But the branch didn't share our humor. It gave another loud *CREAK*. "What other choice do we have?" I yelled.

"COME ON, GUYS, LET GO. TRUST ME."

"You let go first," Gary ordered.

"Me?"

"Yeah."

"But I . . . I don't have my glasses."

"What's that got to do with anything?"

Try as I might I couldn't come up with a good reason.

"COME ON, GUYS, TRUST ME. LET GO."

CREAK

"If I go, you'll follow?" I cried.

"Maybe . . ."

CREAK . . . GROAN . . .

"All right, I'll follow!"

"Promise?"

CREAK . . . GROAN . . . C-R-A-C-K . . .

"ALL RIGHT, ALL RIGHT, I PROMISE!"

I looked back over my shoulder at Dale. He stood there, waist deep in water, arms spread wide.

"COME ON, WALLY, YOU CAN TRUST ME."

And he was right. After all I'd seen and heard this week, I knew I could trust him. So, with a deep breath, I turned to Gary and said, "I get fifty points for going first."

. . . And then I let go.

The current whisked me off like a leaf in a hurricane. Somebody started screaming. It sounded a lot like me. It probably was. After several terrifying seconds, I felt myself crash hard into Dale's chest. *Real* hard.

He gave a loud "OOAAAF!" but wrapped his arms around me so tight I knew he wouldn't let go. Not for the world. Quickly, he half drug, half carried me toward shore where a dozen people grabbed me and tried to make me lie down. But I wasn't in a lying down mood. Gary was still out there. And by the way Dale kept shouting to him, it looked like he'd changed his mind about letting go.

I scrambled to my feet and got as close to the bank as they'd let me. "COME ON, GARY!" I shouted. "COME ON, MAN, YOU PROMISED!"

"I'M BIGGER THAN YOU," he yelled. "HE WON'T BE ABLE TO HANG ON!" There was no missing the panic in Gary's voice.

"I WILL HOLD ON," Dale shouted. "TRUST ME!"

The branch gave another sickening *C-R-A-C-K*. Only this time it meant business. This time it slipped a good foot and a half. Any second it would give out all together. Any second Gary would be swept into the river.

"WALLY?" he shouted. His voice was shaking with fear. "HELP ME, MAN. YOU GOT TO HELP ME!"

"THERE'S NOTHING I CAN DO!" My own voice was breaking as I angrily rubbed the tears from my eyes. "YOU GOT TO TRUST HIM, GARY! YOU GOT TO LET GO!"

"WALLY?"

By now the rest of the camp was joining in. "COME ON, GARY. YOU CAN DO IT, MAN. YOU CAN DO IT!"

"I WON'T LET YOU GO!" Dale promised. "I WON'T LET GO!"

"TRUST HIM, GARY," I cried, "TRUST HIM."

And then Gary did the bravest thing he'd ever done in his life. He let go. He forgot all about the pain and stuff he'd gotten from so many people for so many years. He forgot all of that and put his trust in Dale.

And just in time . . . because the exact moment Gary let go, the branch broke loose.

We all gasped as Gary and the heavy limb thundered toward Dale. Any other guy would have dived out of the way. But Dale had given his word. So he stood there. Gary and the huge, spiked tree limb rushed right at him, but Dale would not move.

Next, everything went kinda in slow motion—like in the movies. I'm sure lots of people were screaming, but I couldn't hear them. I'm sure the river was still roaring, but I couldn't hear it. All I saw was Gary crash into Dale. All I heard was Dale cry out in pain as the big guy slammed into him.

But Dale kept his word. He didn't let go. He wrapped his arms around Gary and held him for dear life.

Then Dale did one other thing. And it's something I'll remember for as long as I live. He saw the limb rushing straight at them and swung Gary behind him, to protect the boy. In one quick move Dale covered Gary and took the full blow of the limb into his own back. He let out an agonizing scream as the wooden spikes tore through his clothes and dug into his body. But he still wouldn't let go.

In a flash, the water was filled with kids and other counselors as we all tugged on the rope to bring Dale and Gary back to shore. Gary was doing fine, though he was bawling like a baby. Come to think of it, so was I. Come to think of it, so were most of us.

But not Dale. Dale was hurting too bad to cry. Dale was also bleeding . . . a lot.

Chapter 11

Wrapping Up

While Gary and I were taking our little afternoon swim, Wall Street had called 911 on her cell phone. By the time we hauled Dale back to the parking lot, an ambulance and fire truck were just pulling in. Everyone was all scared and of course all the girls thought Dale was going to die. Dale tried to tell them he was okay, that he *wasn't* going to die. But that only made them more positive he *was* going to die since that's what dying heroes always say *before* they die.

Anyway, it was dinnertime when the bus finally rolled back into camp. Word came for us that Dale really was going to be okay. He'd gotten some nasty cuts and had bruised a rib or two, but that was about it. Course, that still didn't make anyone jump for joy. I figured that's why no one showed up at the Toxic Waste Site for dinner—no one felt like eating.

But, as usual, I figured wrong.

"Congratulations!" Opera shouted as he plopped down beside me. Even though he'd shut off his Walkman as a symbol of mourning, he was still shouting . . . and eating. Force of habit, I guess.

"Congratulations for what?" I asked, pushing some frozen purple thingies around on my plate.

"According to Wall Street's calculations, you won the competition."

"Oh, that."

"Better hurry, though."

"For what?"

"Jimmy Jack's selling tickets for the rest of the camp to watch."

"Watch?"

"Sure. The Gorilla lost, so he and his Goons have to pick up the trash. Jimmy Jack's selling tickets for everyone to watch them and to listen to your victory speech."

"*Victory* speech?"

"Yup, he says you're really going to lay into ol' Gorilla Man. 'The Speech of a Lifetime,' he calls it."

I rose to my feet pretty steamed. "After all that's happened, he's doing that?" I didn't wait for an answer. I crossed the room and threw open the cafeteria doors. It was exactly like Opera said. There were Gary and his Goons picking up trash all around the ground, and there was Jimmy Jack doing what he did best. . . .

"You there," he shouted at some little kid, "step to the rear. Only front-row tickets here. If you wanna better view, buy a better ticket. Better hurry though, they're going fast!"

I looked back at Gary. He didn't say a word. He just stayed bent over picking up the garbage.

"There he is now!" Jimmy Jack shouted as he spotted me. "The man of the hour!"

All heads turned toward me. The group started to clap as they jostled and pushed me toward the front. Pretty soon they started up their chant: *"Wal-ly, Wal-ly, Wal-ly . . ."*

"This is better than I expected!" Jimmy Jack shouted into my ear as he flashed a handful of bills.

"Speech!" someone shouted. "Give us the speech!" Pretty soon the rest of the group joined in. "Speech, speech, speech!"

I looked at them. They looked at me.

"Speech, speech, speech . . ."

"This is it, man!" Jimmy Jack shouted. "Give 'em both barrels! Make Gorilla Boy sorry he was ever born!"

Finally, everyone settled down. It grew very quiet. I looked over at Gary one last time. He and the Goons were still working away. It took me another minute but finally I made up my mind. Without a word, I turned and walked toward Gary.

"What's he doing?" someone called from the crowd.

I knew exactly what I was doing. Once I was at Gary's side I bent over and started picking up trash.

He glared over at me. "What are you trying to prove, Weasel? *You* won."

"Trust me," I whispered.

Meanwhile, back at the crowd, Jimmy Jack started to sound a little nervous. "Come on, Wally. Come on, man, the joke's over."

But it was no joke. I kept on working. I was through with Jimmy Jack and his games. I was through trying to be something I wasn't. If Jimmy Jack Hucksterly wanted a victory speech, then Jimmy Jack Hucksterly was going to have to make it.

"Hey, this isn't what we paid for," somebody shouted.

"Come on, Wally," Jimmy Jack called a little more urgently. But I ignored him.

Jimmy Jack started to sweat. A lot. He tried to start up the chant, *"Wal-ly, Wal-ly, Wal-ly. . . ."*

But this time, it didn't work. Pretty soon it was being drowned out by complaints.

"You said he was going to lay into him."

"'The Speech of a Lifetime,' you promised!"

"This is lame, man."

"I want my money back."

"Give us our money!"

"Come on, guys," Jimmy Jack called, "I'm sure Wally's got something to say." He turned to me. "Right, Wally? *WALLY?*"

But ol' Wally boy didn't have a word to say. He just kept on working.

"WE WANT OUR MONEY BACK!" the crowd started to shout. "WE WANT OUR MONEY!"

They grew louder by the second. And the louder they grew, the more Jimmy Jack sweated. And the more Jimmy Jack sweated, the more I started smiling.

Luckily, Gary was the only one to spot that smile. At first he just looked at me kind of puzzled like. And then, maybe it was just my imagination, but for the briefest second, it looked like he actually returned it. Of course, the smile vanished as quickly as it appeared. After all, Gary the Gorilla did have a reputation to keep up.

* * * * *

The following morning Dale stood beside our buses as we loaded our gear. He was kind of bandaged up here and there, but for a man who was supposed to have died he looked pretty good.

Of course, Wall Street, Opera, and I said the usual good-byes and made the usual promises to write. I've got to hand it to Wall Street, she was doing a pretty good job of not crying . . . until the girl part of her finally won out.

"By the way," Opera shouted, "what school will you be going to this fall?

"Olympic Heights," I shouted.

"Olympic Heights!" he yelled. "That's where I'm going!"

I couldn't believe my ears. I turned to Wall Street. She was also grinning!

"Not you, too!"

Her grin widened and she nodded.

"Looks like we'll be seeing a lot more of each other!" Opera shouted.

Before I could figure if that was good or bad, some guy from behind yelled, "Let's move it, McDoogle!" and gave me a shove into the bus.

I tried to keep my balance. But the last step sort of threw me. Before I knew it I was flat on my face in the aisle. Of course, everyone laughed and there were the usual "what an idiot" and "way to go, Mc*Dorkel*." But I didn't mind much.

In fact, it was kind of nice to get back into the swing of things.

I looked around and spotted Gary toward the back. As usual, he had the required empty seat beside him. It looked kind of inviting, but I knew better than to join him. It's true, we'd both gone through a lot of changes—especially in the wisdom department. I mean, I learned all about choosing friends, and being kind to others, and not judging someone by how they look and on and on.

And Gary? Well, I can't say for sure. But he definitely learned a lot more about trusting people—and maybe even about trusting God.

Yet, with all of that wisdom, I still didn't think it was such a good idea to sit in his empty seat. I mean, there's also wisdom in not putting yourself in bodily danger, right?

The bus lurched into gear, and I went staggering backward into the nearest empty seat. It was beside a little fifth grade beauty. Hmm, maybe my luck was improving. As an upper-classman in the sixth grade, I figured I'd go ahead and brighten her day by flashing her my famous McDoogle smile. "Hi there," I said.

Her response was exactly as I expected. "Oh gross. Do you, like, really have to sit here?"

It's nice to know some things never change.

Now that the introductions were over and I

had nothing else to do for the rest of the trip, I reached down and pulled Ol' Betsy up to my lap. It'd been a couple of days since I worked on Mutant Man, but as I recall, he and Dr. Ghastly were having a little face-to-face meeting with the ground—at about a zillion miles an hour.

"Quick!" shouts our hero.

"Quick, what?" cries our villain.

"Quick something, we've only got 1.4 seconds before impact." Suddenly, an idea comes to Mutant's marvelous manly mind. "Wait a minute!"

"We don't have a minute, we've only got 1.—"

"The reverse switch! Hit the reverse switch!"

In a flash the Gorilla reaches over to the Wisdom Sucker Upper and switches it to reverse. Immediately, it quits sucking and starts blowing. As the air rushes out of the Sucker Upper's sucker, it slows their fall until they gently float to the earth.

But something else happens. Since the Sucker Upper is no longer sucking but blowing, all that wisdom it had sucked up is pouring out on every-thing and everybody.

Suddenly, mice and cats are playing together, meter maids are putting quarters INTO parking meters, tel-evangelists are begging to GIVE money away, and, most importantly, supern-erds are no longer wearing white socks with black shoes.

Even our hero and bad guy are affected....

"Isn't this just too wonderful," sniffs Dr. Ghastly as he brushes the tears from his eyes, "the way every-body's suddenly so wise?"

"It's truly beautiful," Mutant Man bawls as he blows into his superhero hanky.

"Listen," Gorilla suggests. He throws his big hairy arm around our good guy. "Why don't you come on over to my place for dinner tonight?"

"No kidding?"

"Sure. I'd love for you to meet the family—especially my sister. What a cook! She makes great spaghetti and banana balls. And you'll love her peanut meringue pie."

"Why, that would just be so super-nifty, Doctor."

"Please, call me Ghastly, all my friends do. Oh, and if we hurry, we can catch the last part of *The Brady Bunch*."

"Really? That's my favorite TV show of all time!"

"What a coincidence; mine too! Do you remember the time Peter went around tape-recording Marsha and Cindy and Greg and everybody?"

"Yeah! And then Alice and the kids got together...."

And so the new friends stroll off into the sunset, arm in arm—stronger, kinder, and, most importantly, wiser than ever before.

And yet, somehow we suspect the adventures of our superhero are not quite over. Somehow we know there is other evil in other parts of the galaxy. And somehow we know that wherever evil lurks, there we will find, Ta-Da-DAAA! (there's that good guy music again) the one and only...Mutant Man McDoogle!